Seven Nights with a Scot

SEVEN NIGHTS WITH A SCOT

An All the Kings Men Romance

Gerri Russell

TULE
PUBLISHING

ISBN: 978-1-949707-66-3

Dedication

To Melissa and Anna

Thank you for all the smiles, laughter, and hugs you give so generously. My life is enriched by you both.

PROLOGUE

Edinburgh Castle, Scotland
December 1st, 1590

"LADY SINCLAIR, THE king wishes tae see you."

Vivian Sinclair looked up from her worktable. The footman she knew as Andrew watched her from the doorway of her work chamber belowstairs near the kitchen. He never came inside the room. It was as though he feared, like so many of the other servants in the castle, he might somehow be affected by whatever herbal remedy she created. Potions, they called them with shuttered eyes.

"I haven't finished my tisane for His Grace yet." Vivian didn't bother to hide her confusion as she continued to grind the willow bark into a powder with her mortar and pestle. "Only a few minutes more."

"The king said the matter was urgent and I was tae bring you straight tae him," Andrew said, easing away from the doorway as she set her pestle down. He watched with a patient face as she wiped her hands on her apron.

Vivian tried to hide the shaking of her hands as she removed her apron. She took a moment to smooth away from her cheeks the fiery-red locks that escaped her ribbon. She knew all too well the look of displeasure that would come to King James VI's face the moment he saw her.

She did not resemble the noblewoman she was or even a lady of fashion. Her wild hair could never be tamed into the ringlets that were so popular among the other courtiers and she hated wearing it up; her gown was simple, unadorned and several years out of date. Vivian didn't wear the fine dresses the king, her guardian, had had made for her, preferring to wear things she didn't fear soiling when she tended her patients instead. "Do you have any idea what this is about?" she asked as she followed Andrew up the main staircase.

Andrew wouldn't meet her gaze. "He dinna say. But his mood is rather foul."

"Thank you for the warning," Vivian said as she stifled a spurt of dread. Why did the king want to see her now? She had attended him earlier this morning and had been crafting a tisane to help ease the pain in his joints. The pains came over him ever since his return from Denmark with his wife, Anne. Or could he have finally heard the whispers that had started last week after she had cured Lady MacPhearson's fever? The older woman had been pleased but her husband had called Vivian's abilities nothing less than witchcraft. No matter the reason, the king wanting to see her for a second time in one day did not bode well for her.

Vivian and Andrew walked in silence until they came to

the doorway of the great hall. Andrew bowed to her there and remained at the door while she entered. The opulent chamber was one of the king's favorites with its magnificent wooden ceiling, paneled wainscoting, and red walls. Standing tall, she continued toward the massive fireplace where the king sat alone. He looked up when she stopped before him. "Vivian."

"Your Grace." She bowed and placed a grateful kiss upon the hand he extended to her, as was proper. "You wished to see me again, my lord?"

As she suspected, an irritated scowl came to his face as he took in her tidy but rather plain form of dress. "I can no longer put off my duty as your guardian. We need to discuss your impending marriage."

"My what?" Vivian gasped. She reached with an unsteady hand for the chair beside the king, wilting into it. Even though marriage was expected of young women, such a state was the last thing she wanted.

"I believe you heard me." Leaning back in his chair, King James appraised her. "I've betrothed you to a very dear friend of mine, Laird Dugald Campbell. He is a seasoned lord, and he will be good to you, my child."

Vivian clutched the arms of the chair. Her mother and father's marriage had been no love match, arranged by James's father as a means to join two estates in a consolidation of power between two clans. Her parents had tried to make their marriage work, but they were too dissimilar. Her father had been strong and domineering, great strengths on the battlefield but those same traits followed him home during times of peace. As the years went by, her mother became fearful and dispirited, slowly becoming a shell of the woman she'd once been—a woman with no heart, no happiness, and no will to live. Vivian had always feared something similar might happen to her.

And yet her fears were of little concern to the king. He wanted her married. She had little choice in the matter. "What do you mean by 'seasoned'?" she asked, unable to hide the slight tremor in her voice.

Hearing her fear, the king sighed. "A mature man has a lot to offer you, Vivian. He is settled in his ways. He already has an heir. He will welcome your skills as a healer. And, while this is no love match, I know, he and his clan will protect you from . . ."

The king did not finish his sentence but she already knew what he meant to say. The witch hunting that had been rampant in Denmark had followed him back to Scotland through his own fears of the unknown.

"Darkness is coming, and I fear I may not be able to protect you here at court any longer. You are too different, too vulnerable, and I will not sacrifice you because of something I can no longer ignore."

Vivian shook her head, trying to clear her chaotic thoughts. "You do not have to believe what others believe. Witchcraft is not real. You are an intelligent man. Look at the facts. Look at things logically. I do not understand—"

"You do not have to understand," the king said brusquely. His face reddened.

Not many at court would have talked to him in such a fashion, but she had to make him see some sense. "Witches are not real."

His eyes flared. "I am your king and I know what is real and what is not." A moment later he settled back in his chair with a sigh. "Why must you always challenge me? You are very like your dear father, you are."

"I mean you no disrespect, my lord. I care about you as I would have my own father."

"And I care about you, Vivian. Trust that I am doing the right thing for you. To protect you just as your father once protected me. I owe him that much."

She'd heard the tale many times of how her father had placed himself in harm's way in order to save the king's life. It was ultimately how she'd ended up as a ward of the king after her mother's death. The king had been nothing but kind to her over the past six years. Even so, she knew the king's kindness would not last forever, especially now that he had taken a wife himself. Vivian had been of an age to marry for years. It was a miracle he hadn't tried to marry her off before now.

"You leave tomorrow for Kilkerran. Pack only the supplies you cannot replace. And never speak about your visions to anyone ever again. Do you understand?"

She drew a breath, trying to slow her wildly beating heart. "My visions have been helpful to you. I helped you avoid an assassination attempt. I predicted your marriage to Anne of Denmark. I revealed you would see eight children born into this world, and that you would not only become king of Scotland, but England as well."

Vivian stood, no longer able to contain her agitation. "I predicted your mother's death. And foretold of your success as a scholar, and that it would be you who made the words of the Bible accessible to not only the nobility, but the common man as well."

"It is hard to know what is true when so many things have yet to transpire." The king frowned. "Have you seen any future attempts on my life?"

"If I do have such visions, I promise to warn you, Your Grace."

After a moment he went on. "You did predict my marriage to Anne, but you failed to tell me about the attempt on her life by the others of your kind."

Her kind? The words stalled her pacing. King James had never addressed her as such before. He'd always referred to her as his secret informant and healer in the past. Never as a witch. He had heard the whispers Laird MacPhearson had started.

"You will punish me for a crime that happened so far away and months ago?" Vivian had heard the stories from other courtiers who claimed witches had tried to harm the queen as she sailed from Denmark to Scotland to meet her new husband. King James had gone to the queen's rescue and the couple had arrived back in Scotland safely.

"I am not the instigator of this madness," the king said, his tone defensive. "Even I cannot stop what is coming. There is unrest among my subjects. Plagues and crop failures are straining communities across Scotland. In response, people are looking for someone to blame. This time they are blaming witches. A tribunal has been established in North Berwick for several men and women accused of witchery. I must go and observe before things get too out of control, but not until I know you are safe and in the care of my old friend."

"Surely you have younger friends," she quipped, then held her tongue at the king's sharp look.

"Only you get away with such talk, I assure you. Now stop arguing with me and do as I command. I trust Laird Campbell with your life. That should be enough."

Vivian shivered, fighting the unease that had settled inside her. "By sending me away, you are in essence labeling me a witch. Is that what I am to you?"

"Shhh," the king admonished, his gaze shifting around the still-empty chamber. "Mind your tongue. Others might not see things the way I do. While my word is absolute, do as I say or you may yet find yourself in danger."

Was that a threat or a promise?

Regardless, her life was about to change dramatically. For

the better or the worse remained unknown. This was one of those times when she wished she could see into her own future, but those glimpses were never forced.

Vivian straightened to give the king a single nod of acquiescence. As the king's witch, she had no choice but to do as he bid.

KING JAMES WATCHED Vivian retreat from the great hall. When he was alone, he released his grip on the arms of his chair. Flexing his hands, he eased the tension that had built there while he and his ward had talked. James was obliged to settle the girl somewhere. After all, he'd promised her father on his deathbed that he'd keep her safe.

With her gone, he could now focus on his own safety. James's chest felt so tight he could not breathe but he forced his fear aside. For too long he had lived with the knowledge that Satan was trying to destroy him. It was time to turn the tides in the king's favor and rid the country of that monster's demons. To assure his own safety, he'd gathered Scotland's finest warriors to his side, men who had vowed to protect him. His magnificent seven. His greatest triumph. His greatest secret against any threat.

He had considered sending Vivian to one of them, but he could not risk lessening his own defenses for her sake. He needed all of the seven focused on protecting their king.

Instead, he'd had no choice but to send his ward to the farthest western corner of Scotland. The once great Laird Dugald Campbell would protect the girl and fulfill the king's obligation to her father.

For an instant, James's confidence faltered. Vivian was so young, and his friend was ill. One of the seven would be a better choice, and yet Dugald desperately needed Vivian's special abilities as a healer to prolong his life.

James inhaled slowly, then let the air slide from his lungs. His decision would stand. There'd be no more doubts. He would send Vivian to a place where no one would suspect her of anything other than being a wife caring for her elderly husband. With care, Dugald could survive for many years, meaning Vivian would be safe as long as Rupert Campbell, the laird's only son, stayed away from Kilkerran.

Rupert Campbell's role as sheriff of Haddingtonshire on the opposite side of the country had kept him away from home for years. And now, as leader of the witch hysteria sweeping the country, Rupert would be out of Vivian's reach for years to come. James had granted Rupert the power to do whatever to whomever he needed as long as it was directed at ridding the country of evil. James had no desire to hunt for witches himself. His part in all of this would be more that of an academic observer. He would watch things unfold and record the results. Men like Rupert Campbell would see that those accused were hunted down and brought to justice.

As Vivian's guardian, he would do all he could to keep

her out of Rupert's way. She was an innocent in all of this, he had decided years ago. He knew her to be honest and God-fearing. Her skill with herbs as well as her visions were a divine gift and not something to be feared, even though others with similar talents might be touched by evil and therefore fittingly should not be spared.

James shifted his gaze to the flames devouring the wood in the hearth before him. Fire: the source of warmth, purification, and destruction. Just like him, the people of Scotland were frightened—frightened enough to give a man like Rupert Campbell the power to do as he wished in order to protect them, to find traitors in their midst, and rid their homeland of evil.

Rubbing his forehead against the burgeoning ache building there, James turned away from the fire and moved to the door. There was work to be done. He'd returned to Edinburgh with his bride, ready to accept the burdens of guiding his realm through these dangerous times. Now was not the time to start second-guessing himself or the players he'd set in motion.

If he were going to make changes to Scottish society and the world at large, he must release a proclamation to rid Scotland of all sorcery and work with men like Rupert Campbell to see the job done. Whether he wanted to or not.

Lives would be lost—some of them innocent—when the hunting of witches began. He'd done what he could to protect Vivian. Her future was now in Dugald Campbell's hands.

CHAPTER ONE

Kilkerran, Scotland
June 1591

A S EARLY MORNING light filtered into the laird's bed-chamber, Vivian Sinclair Campbell took her dying husband's hand in her own, wrapping her youthful fingers around his gnarled ones. Their half-year-old marriage was one of convenience, and by tomorrow even that would come to an end if the sound of his labored breathing were any indication.

Laird Dugald Campbell had had a good life. A long life. This moment should not be a mournful one, yet she was sad. Sad that she was the only one who would sit at his bedside as he drew each agonizing breath. Sad that she could do nothing more for him with her herbs and poultices. Sad that once he took his final breath she would have no further protection from the once-great Laird Campbell or even his clan. She would be back to where she started—a woman alone in a world of manipulative men.

Her current situation was proof as to why it was important to keep herself free of entanglements such as marriage and children. How could she shield an innocent child from the horrors of this world when she could not secure her own safety?

It had been six long months since King James sent her to Kilkerran to marry his old friend. Despite the fact the match was more advantageous to Dugald, the king had promised the old laird would protect her. In his own way, he had. But confined to his bed as he'd been for the past fortnight, he did not see or hear the growing hysteria his own son Rupert—known across the land as the Witch Hunter of Scotland—caused throughout the country in his search for the unnatural.

Vivian's stomach knotted at the thought Rupert might return home soon as news reached him of his father's impending death. When he did, any illusion of safety her current situation had created would be gone.

Dugald stirred, suddenly restless in his sleep. He tossed his head back and forth. Vivian brought a cool compress to his temple. "I'm here," she said softly as she smoothed the cloth across his brow.

He turned toward her and opened his eyes. Six months ago, when she'd first arrived at Kilkerran, those eyes had been filled with not only compassion but also strength. Over the months, that strength had faded. There were some at the castle who blamed her for that change. They didn't trust the tisanes she mixed for their laird to drink each morning.

The truth was, without her medicines Dugald would

have died months ago. His heart was failing and fluid filled his lungs, making it difficult to breathe. They'd all expected a miracle from her upon her arrival. What she'd been able to offer her new husband had been relief from his symptoms, but there was no cure for the damage to such vital organs. "Is there anything I can do to make you more comfortable?"

He offered her the hint of a smile. "Ye did yer best, Wife. Now there's nothin' either of us can do but wait fer the end."

"I'm sorry."

"'Tis not yer fault. I'm the one who's failed ye, my dear. I was tae protect ye from everyone, including my own people. They do nae understand and I fear Rupert will nae arrive in time to set things right before—" A spasmodic cough racked Dugald's body.

Rupert. Dugald either did not want to acknowledge or truly did not know about his son's reputation. Vivian feared she would never receive the protection her husband wanted from his son. "Do not concern yourself with me. I'll find a way forward." Vivian lifted her husband's torso into a more upright position, trying to make it easier for him to fill his lungs with air.

He took the cloth from her hands and coughed into it, spotting the white linen with a deep red.

The end was close.

Vivian's eyes burned and her throat tightened. She did not love her husband as a wife should, but she did care for him. He had not been as overpowering as her own father had been to her mother, giving evidence that not all marriages were as theirs had been. And yet, her husband's son had added deadly complications to Dugald's past three marriages.

Vivian had never met Dugald's only child, but she'd heard rumors among the castle residents that Rupert was responsible for his father's previous wives' demises, even that of his own mother. Vivian felt a cold touch on her neck, made from dire whispers and haunted eyes when those who knew Rupert spoke of the man.

When Dugald's coughing fit ended, he collapsed back against the pillows. "My last and final wish was tae see Rupert and beg him tae protect ye."

Chances were Rupert would do nothing to assist his father's fourth wife. "I'm sure he will make every effort to come home, Dugald," she said, the words at odds with her own worries. "Why not rest for a while, build up your strength for when he arrives?"

With a weak nod, Dugald closed his eyes and drifted off to sleep. Vivian settled back in her chair, determined to wait beside her husband until the old laird simply slipped away.

Vivian must have drifted off to sleep herself because a steady knock on the chamber door startled her awake. "Enter," she said, straightening her gown.

Gillis, her maid, slipped into the chamber, shutting the door softly behind her. Worry etched into every line on the older woman's face. "Milady, I've come tae warn ye. Rupert's here. He'll be up any moment tae see his father. What should we do?"

"Nothing," Vivian replied, coming to her feet, quelling the surge of fear that tightened her chest. "He ought to come up."

"I'm worried fer yer safety, milady. Rupert's not a kind man." Gillis moved to the bedside and took Vivian's hands in her own. The woman had been hired to the castle especially for Vivian at her marriage to Dugald. In the last six months, the two had grown very close, close enough to speak their minds without reserve. "The other servants have nae love fer the master's son. Some of the things they say about him—"

"At the moment we must think of Dugald and his needs. Rupert is his son and he wishes to make his peace there. That is more important than anything else," Vivian interrupted, trying to reassure the worried maid.

Gillis frowned. "M'lady, have a care. The man is nae good."

Before Vivian could reply, the door to the chamber opened.

"Where is he?"

A tall man with dark red hair and a hawk-like gaze stepped into the chamber. She'd heard Rupert was a commanding figure, but the reality of the man was far more imposing than she'd imagined. Vivian curtsied. "Welcome home, Rupert. Your father has been asking for you."

He came to a sudden stop at the sight of his father, lying

almost lifeless in the bed. Rupert brought a hand up to cover his mouth. "Is it consumption? Is he contagious?"

As Gillis retreated to the shadows of the chamber, Vivian shook her head, wishing she, too, could remove herself from Rupert's overpowering presence. "I do not believe so on either account. Many of us have been in direct contact with him and none have fallen ill," Vivian replied.

Rupert's eyes narrowed on her. "Then what have you done to him? Last I saw my father he was hale and hearty."

"That was five years ago by your father's account. His illness has taken a toll on him over the years."

"Nay. This advance into illness is too swift. It can't be natural." Rupert dropped onto the bed at his father's side. "If my father knew he was failing, he would have sent me a message."

Dugald's eyes fluttered open. "As I recall, I sent ye several." He stared at his son for a long moment before a faint smile came to his lips. "Ye came this time. That's what matters."

Instead of expressing remorse, Rupert's face darkened with anger. "My work keeps me busy. In the last two weeks alone I've detained fourteen witches for the tribunal." His gaze shifted to Vivian.

She flinched at the palpable hatred in his dark eyes.

Triumph lit his features. "I sense something of the dark arts at work here, through the efforts of this witch whom you call wife."

Dugald frowned. In a sudden surge of strength, he clasped his gnarled fingers around his son's arm. "There is nae truth tae that. Mark my words, Son. Vivian has helped me more than ye can know in these last few months. I'll die in peace instead of agony thanks tae her."

"She's bewitched you." Rupert shook off his father's grip as he stood, pacing back and forth at the bedside. "You have no idea what sorcery is at work here."

"Nae, Son," Dugald wheezed. "'Tis ye who are mistaken. Vivian is kind and generous. I'll nae have ye malign her in such a way." He started coughing—long, protracted hacking that shook his entire frame.

The sight of his father suffering seemed to defuse Rupert's anger. His shoulders slumped. "I did not come here to fight."

Vivian sat beside her husband and poured him a cup of the ivy leaf tisane she had brewed earlier. She offered Dugald a small sip, then another. The liquid soothed his coughing and he settled back against the bed once more.

"I need . . . a promise . . . from ye," Dugald forced out.

Rupert's eyes narrowed. "I'll hear you out, but with no guarantees."

"As ye become the head of the Campbell clan, I need ye tae care for Vivian as I have cared for her. Protect her with yer life. Accept her as a Campbell, then the others will too," he said in a surprisingly strong voice. He met his son's steely gaze with his own.

"You ask the impossible."

Vivian shivered at the hardness in Rupert's voice.

"Why?" Dugald asked as his strength suddenly faltered. "I canna go tae my maker . . . in peace without yer word."

Rupert stopped pacing, his look incredulous. "You, more than anyone, know why I do what I do."

"Yer mother was nae a witch. She was . . . misguided."

"Misguided?" Rupert spat the word. "I believe you mean evil. She wanted us both dead."

"Being unhappy . . . doesn't make a person evil."

Rupert turned away, glancing about the chamber. From her position on the bed Vivian could see his profile. The muscles of his jaw clenched then released. Finally, he turned back to look at her. "I'm both unhappy and determined, and I'll continue to be so until every witch in this country is dead. If that includes your current wife, then so be it."

"Rupert, nay—" Dugald's words cut off as a fit of coughing seized his lungs.

Instead of tending her husband, Vivian stood and approached Rupert. She whispered, "Please, I beg you to lie to him. Say whatever he wants you to say to ease his way from this world."

Menace darkened his features. "Tell an untruth?"

Vivian refused to back down. "Have some respect for your father. The truth matters little. Let his soul leave this world in peace."

"And after he dies?" Rupert asked, his gaze intensifying

on her.

She cast a glance back at Dugald as spasmodic coughing rattled his frame. "Then you and I can come to terms of our own."

"My terms will be when you burn at the stake," Rupert said, his voice rough and sharp.

She held back a shiver as she turned to face him once more. "I am the king's ward. He'll never allow you to harm me."

"Is that a challenge?"

"Whatever happens after your father is gone will be between the two of us. For now, please put his mind at rest. He needs your compliance, truthful or not."

The corner of Rupert's mouth lifted. "If that is what you wish, then that is what I shall do," he said, stepping past her toward his father.

With their two heads close, their whispers could not reach her ears, but she hoped Rupert would be true to his word for his father's sake. Even though he had done as she'd asked, Vivian's stomach heaved. She wished she could have had a vision of this moment, something, anything to prepare her for what was to come. But her visions were never that convenient.

Gillis emerged from the shadows. She grasped Vivian by the arms. "What did ye do, m'lady?"

"What had to be done." This time Vivian could not stop the shiver that cascaded through her. Her morality would put her own life at risk. But any other choice would be unthinkable.

"The moment m'laird dies that man will be after ye."

Vivian nodded.

"Run. Go now while ye still have a chance."

Vivian turned to watch the two men talking, their heads close, their words muted. "I cannot leave until Dugald does."

"By then it will be too late," Gillis said, her tone filled with anguish.

"It's a chance I must take for Dugald's sake." She'd come to Kilkerran at the king's urging and with his promise that she would be safe from a world of people who misunderstood her gift. But she wasn't safe. She had a feeling she would never be safe again.

DUGALD DIED SHORTLY after sunrise the next morning. Vivian had helped the end come peacefully, burning thyme at his bedside to ease each labored breath. She'd done her duty to her husband, but now it was time for her to slip silently from the castle before anyone noticed her absence. She'd packed her most precious herbs and supplies in a pouch that she'd tied at her waist. Using the back stairs and staying hidden in the shadows, she slipped from the castle and made her way to the village just beyond the castle gates.

Gray rainclouds hovered overhead, making the morning

sky appear darker than usual. Last night she'd considered taking a horse, then decided against it. A horse would make it easier for Rupert to track her. She had funds to pay for a seat on a coach.

No matter how she accomplished it, she needed to disappear.

Vivian reached the outskirts of the large village and continued down one of its many narrow streets. When she came to Mary Tate's house, she paused. A week ago, Mary Tate had delivered her baby several weeks earlier than anticipated. Despite being small, the child had appeared healthy and had started nursing within hours after the birth. Vivian forced herself to move on. Her patients would be well enough without her.

On the next street she passed by the house where Billy Abbott lived with his parents. It had been three days since the youth had fallen from a ledge and broken several bones. His fall should have killed him, yet Vivian had been able to reset his bones and stanch the bleeding, saving his life.

There were so many more whom she had helped. Yet now that she needed help, she could ask no one to assist her or they would also fall victim to Rupert's unreasoning wrath.

Continuing on, Vivian passed a row of thatched houses, then skirted the edge of the marketplace, staying on the fringes, away from the villagers engaged in their morning routines. She pulled the hood of her cloak more tightly against her face and followed a worn dirt path up a hillside.

The sound of horses plodding through mud and the soft patter of footsteps came to her as she neared the heart of the village. She hitched up her skirts to climb over a low wall, and emerged on the main street of town. She had barely settled on both feet when pain assailed her temples. She drew a sharp breath as a vision thundered through her mind.

A boy, playing near the roadway. A large black horse galloping. Hooves coming down, sharp edges flying. The child's scream blending with the horse's. Pain. Blood. Death.

A heartbeat later Vivian's vision cleared, bringing her back to the moment. As she had for years, Vivian had glimpsed a possible future. Overly aware of her surroundings, the incongruous sweet scent of springtime heather assailed her senses. Nausea roiled in her stomach. Lethargy attacked her arms and legs, but she forced herself to straighten. She must not give in to the toll the visions took on her body. She had to keep moving toward the forest.

At the cost of a young boy's life?

Vivian swallowed around the lump in her throat. Saving him could cost her everything, but there was no other choice. Lifting her heavy skirts, she hurried down the rain-dampened main road that ran through the village of Kilkerran. Her breath left whispers of mist in the morning air. Frantically, she searched for the blond-haired child. Instead she saw the people she'd come to know over the past six months as they paused in their daily chores and activities to study her with narrowed, suspicious eyes. A shiver of ice slid down her spine as she hurried past.

Not long ago the villagers had been grateful for her abilities as a healer and her strange way of knowing what the future would bring. Now when she looked at them she only saw fear. The witch trials had fueled suspicions of anyone who was different or did things that were unexplained.

To avoid any confrontation, Vivian hurried her steps. She turned a corner near the blacksmith's shop, felt the rush of heat from his forge against her already-flushed skin. The smithy was as careful as Vivian not to draw attention to his skills. She'd heard the villagers' whispers, accusing him of mastering the dark arts as he mixed iron with bone dust to form hardened steel.

Why did others not see their talents were a gift instead of something to be feared?

The creeping sensation of being watched again raised the hairs at Vivian's nape. Even her kinship with the king couldn't save her if she were publicly accused of misdeeds. He'd sent her away six months ago in order to protect himself and his new bride from any association with her. But the king had been wrong about her finding obscurity in Kilkerran.

News of King James's participation in the North Berwick witch trials and the execution of seven witches had reached even the smallest towns in Scotland. In its wake, a storm of fear and maliciousness was spreading, sweeping up the wicked and the innocent with equal fervor.

Vivian forced the thoughts aside as she finally caught sight of the boy from her vision in the middle of the road ahead. She raced toward him, dodging the villagers who crowded the street.

In the distance, the steady pounding of horses' hooves thundered. The sound fragmented and exploded in her mind. Three horses rounded the bend, a monstrous black beast in the lead. Two red horses followed behind.

Unaware, the little boy scampered back and forth across the roadway on his hobbyhorse, a look of cheerful abandon on his innocent face. Did no one else hear the horses approach? Did no one else realize the danger?

Her stomach pitched. She tried to call out, but her voice failed her. Desperate to cover the distance that separated her from the child, Vivian surged forward, uncaring of the gasps and stares of the others. She stumbled and fell to her knees and then was up again, running faster.

She reached the child just as the horses did. Cocooning the child with her arms, she threw her weight to the side as they fell. Pain raked across her arm as a hoof came down. A cry escaped her lips.

Crack.

Vivian clutched the child to her chest, hoping to absorb the impact as they hit the rocky ground. Had one of them broken a bone?

The golden-haired boy in her arms appeared unharmed. His blue eyes filled with bewilderment, then relief—until he saw the broken hobbyhorse in his hand. Tears welled in his eyes. His wail of sorrow mixed with the cacophony of sounds—the pounding hooves as they came to a stop, the shouts of men, a shriek of "my son!"

A broken hobbyhorse, not a bone. Vivian struggled to catch her breath. She released her grip on the boy. Her vision clouded and her stomach roiled. The throbbing of her arm matched that of her heartbeat. She clutched her arm only to have a sticky wetness ooze through her fingers.

Vivian knew she should get up and run. Run as far away as she could. This event had been witnessed by too many people for it to go unnoticed by Rupert. He would now know she'd left the castle and intended to escape his grasp. Her only hope was to stay ahead of him. She had to get up. She had to keep running.

The sound of boots from the direction of the snorting horses hit the muddy road, coming toward her. Fear rushed through her, churning her stomach, making her mouth dry. She squinted up into the morning light to see a tall silhouette above her.

"What were you doing in the road with that child?" the man asked in a harsh voice.

Vivian tried to stand, but her legs collapsed beneath her as the vision had sapped her strength. She needed a few moments more to shake off the effects. Then she would disappear. She'd planned to return to the convent where she'd lived with her mother after her father's death and before James had found her. At the convent, her mother had found happiness and healing. Vivian's childhood there had been filled with the same. Perhaps she could return to those happier times as well as find the seclusion she needed to be safe.

"What's wrong with you?" the man beside her asked, bringing her back to the moment. He reached for her uninjured arm and lifted her to her feet. His gaze sharpened.

"What's wrong with me? Your recklessness is at fault here. Did you not see that child playing with his hobby-horse?" She jerked backward, afraid his intelligent gaze might see what others missed.

Before she could move farther away, he reached for her other arm, pulling her hand away from her wound. "Whose blood is this?" His dark gaze shifted from her face to the boy who stood wrapped in his mother's arms. The other villagers circled her. People she knew. People she'd cared for. Though now she hardly recognized them. Their faces had twisted into masks of fear. Fear of her and the unknown.

Vivian shivered. She had expected this moment was coming, and now there was no escape.

William Abbott detached himself from the crowd. He held a dagger in his hands. "It's the Devil's blood. You're a witch."

Vivian swallowed roughly as her gaze flicked between the blade held by a man she once thought of as a friend and the stranger before her. Sweet Mary, she didn't want to die today.

"The blood is mine. It's red, like yours." The world swayed before her eyes. She had to stay in control. She had to find a way out of this situation. Perhaps if she broke through the crowd that pushed toward her and just kept running . . .

She took a step only to have darkness edge her vision. The hand on her arm tightened, keeping her upright. The roar of her blood filled her ears, deafening her to her surroundings. She cried out and looked up into a pair of dark brown eyes. Strong, hard arms wrapped around her.

The stranger stared at her for a moment as something like recognition flared in the depths of his eyes. Impossible. She'd spent most of her life in isolation, hiding . . . The thought faded as her vision swam before her eyes.

"You're right. I was at fault here. I should have been more careful. Let me help you," a deep voice whispered close to her ear.

The tone reverberated in her mind as the world closed in around her. Darkness edged into her field of vision until there was nothing more.

CHAPTER TWO

W HEN VIVIAN ROUSED, it was night. Yet she wasn't in darkness. The soft glow of candlelight threw yellow-gold patterns on the walls and ceiling around her. She was inside, but where? Had the villagers captured her? Was she imprisoned? Her fingers crept to the fresh bandages on her arm. Someone had tended her wound. Her arm still throbbed, but the worst of the slashing pain was no more.

Her mind raced as she searched for answers even though the world around her slowed. She sat up and braced her hands against the quilt beneath her. A sharp pain fired through her arm a moment before it dulled. It was then she noticed a familiar taste on her tongue. Saffron and nutmeg. Whoever had treated her wound had given her laudanum.

Over the years when she'd been given the sleeping draught, it often made her visions come more frequently. She drew a deep breath, forcing her mind to clear. She had to stay in control in order to figure out her situation. After another deep breath, she focused on her immediate sur-roundings.

She was on a bed and dressed in the same gown she'd

worn earlier today, but whose bed? Certainly not her own with its coarse wool blanket. The room she was in was clean and somewhat sparse—with only a bed, a wooden chest near the wall, and a water basin with a pitcher near the bedside. From beyond the one small window she could hear the soft neighing of horses, the rattle of a harness, and the unmistakable sound of horses' hooves against the packed earth. A coaching inn?

What had happened? Suddenly in a rush, images cascaded through her mind. She remembered feeling closed in by the crowd. She saw the horror on their faces. Then strong arms had come around her and a deep voice had rung in her ears.

Was the dark stranger nearby? He obviously hadn't taken her to any of the makeshift gaols that had been set up across the country for those accused of witchcraft. She'd heard enough whispers about those places to know they were nothing like where she was now. Where exactly was she?

Nerves jittering in the pit of her stomach, Vivian slipped off the mattress. Once she was certain her legs held solid despite the laudanum she'd been given, she moved to the window. Pushing the shutters aside, she peered into the darkness. Moonlight spilled across the muddy streets of the village she knew all too well, painting Kilkerran in an eerie light.

Muffled in the shadows below her window, she could hear the sound of men's voices, yet she couldn't make out what they said. In the distance she heard the familiar roar of the waves slamming against the cliffs near the castle. She knew this place. The stranger had taken her to The Old Cross coaching inn just at the edge of the village. The very thought that Rupert was nearby sent her heart into a fast-paced rhythm. Was he behind this? Did the dark stranger work for the new laird of the Campbell clan?

Closing the shutters, Vivian turned and crept toward the door. She wasn't as interested in the answers to her questions as she was in escaping her current situation. Twice this day she'd put herself in danger: refusing to leave Kilkerran before Dugald had died and again when the little boy's life was at stake. It was time to put her own needs first. She had to leave before she found herself in an inescapable situation.

Silently, she pressed the latch down. The door cracked open. A sliver of light distorted her vision. Once her eyes adjusted to the flickering light, she could see the hallway was empty. She opened the door fully and started toward the stairs that most likely led to the common room below.

"I wouldn't go any farther if I were you."

Vivian spun around at the sound of the voice. Dizzy from the motion, she reached for the wall to steady herself. If only they hadn't drugged her.

When her vision cleared, she saw a man stood on the opposite side of her doorway. Well over six feet tall, he looked rugged, dangerous, and all too familiar. Dark brown hair hung to his shoulders, his broad chest was covered with a muslin shirt, and dark breeches clung to his muscular thighs. His arms were folded across his chest and his dark eyes were fixed on her.

"You took me away from the crowd."

"Aye." He raked his hand through his hair, leaving it in disarray. Black stubble covered his strong square jaw.

"Why?" she asked, unsettled by the disturbing warmth that came to her cheeks. "Not that I'm not grateful, but why would you do that for a stranger?"

"You're no stranger," he replied, his deep voice rumbling in the silence that surrounded them. Again, a flash of recognition flared in his eyes.

"I don't know you."

His expression softened. He took a step toward her and Vivian instinctively backed up. She was too far from the stairs to try to escape. And the effects of the laudanum still slowed her movements. He would overtake her before she reached the first stair.

"You have nothing to fear from me." He came to a stop before her and reached out to touch the sleeve of her gown, never taking his eyes off her.

Vivian drew in a sharp breath and let it slide through her lungs. Fear wasn't what sent her pulse racing and yet she could honestly say she was terrified. "Who are you?"

"Quinn Douglas."

Douglas. A clan from the eastern part of Scotland. So why was he in Kilkerran? She frowned. "Your name tells me nothing about who you are or why you helped me." She remembered the crowd closing in on her, heard them accusing her of being a witch.

"I helped you because you were injured. An injury I caused."

She ignored how soft his eyes had gone. "You weren't afraid of what the villagers called me?"

He laughed. "Would a witch sacrifice herself for the sake of a child?"

Her intent was always to help people as the nuns had helped her after the death of both her father and mother. Today, the tables had turned. This man had helped her, and even after William Abbott had called her a witch.

"Thank you. Your help was unexpected." She scrubbed her hands across the lower half of her arms in a futile attempt to rid herself of the sudden chill that permeated her body. "Yet I wonder, why did you do it?"

Quinn's mouth tipped to one side in a smile that lived and died in an instant. He moved closer, until she was no more than an arm's reach away. "I'm not the kind of man to leave a woman to fend for herself in such a situation." His deep voice was impossible to ignore.

"I am grateful," she said honestly. Something in his eyes told her he was not like the others. Still, trusting people was dangerous. The hysteria was very real. Witch hunters actively pursued women and even some men. And God help those who were captured.

"Do you have any family nearby?" he asked.

She shook her head. Rupert was family, but she wasn't safe anywhere near him. Nor was she safe in the village or at this inn. She knew the suspicious old innkeeper wouldn't keep the news of her presence at his inn secret for long. Once the villagers learned Quinn had taken her there, no one in her presence would be safe either. The man before her had no idea what kind of danger threatened people like her. He'd done his good deed. Soon he'd be on his way. At least that was her fervent hope.

"What brings you to Kilkerran in such a hurry?" She stepped back through the doorway of her temporary room, trying to put some distance between them. Only when she was bathed in golden candlelight once more did she realize her mistake. She'd left herself with no escape.

Quinn followed her inside. "Business at Kilkerran Castle."

"What manner of business?" Her breath hitched.

"The king's business." His voice dropped several notches. "He knew your husband was dying."

A shiver went down her spine. How did the king so quickly know such things? "Laird Campbell died only this morning."

"I'm sorry for your loss," Quinn said with sincerity.

A lump formed in Vivian's throat. She'd had no time to grieve this morning and she certainly didn't have time to do so now, yet despite her best efforts to forestall her emotions, tears formed in her eyes. "Rupert Campbell is now laird of Kilkerran and the Campbell clan. He can assist you with the king's business now that Dugald is gone."

"My business is with you, Lady Campbell. Vivian."

Vivian's tears vanished as fear knotted her stomach. He knew who she was. "What manner of business is that?"

"The king has arranged your betrothal to my brother. You are a gift from the king for Reid's service to the crown."

"A gift?" She nearly choked on the words. "I am not some trinket that can be passed from one party to another."

"Your betrothal agreement says otherwise."

Her lungs constricted, making it hard to breathe as she stared at the man before her. As a widow Vivian had hoped she could now control her own destiny. That destiny did not include submitting herself to a second marriage. Dugald had expected nothing of her but companionship and healing. A younger man would demand so much more including a physical relationship, acquiescence, and children. It was her father's insistence of total obedience that had done her mother irreparable harm. She would not be a victim herself, subjected to the bidding of another. Lifting her chin, she said, "Nay. My duty to the king is done. He cannot ask anything more of me."

"You're still a subject of the crown." Quinn's mouth fixed in a grim slash. He took her uninjured arm in a firm grip. "If the king decides you shall marry again, that's exactly what you'll do."

Vivian pulled free from his grasp. Quickly she moved to one side so he couldn't reach for her again. The fear she tasted was dark and bitter. "What if I refuse?"

"Then you would leave me no choice but to force you to do so."

She stared up at him as the candlelight shimmered across his features, giving him a shadowy, dangerous look that sent a shiver through her. He would force her; she had no doubt.

"My brother, Reid, is my twin. I can attest to the fact that he is not only younger than your late husband, he has grown quite adept at protecting the things that matter to him."

"How can I matter to him if he did not come to retrieve me himself?" Her voice was sharp but she didn't care.

"The king did not travel to Denmark initially to retrieve his new bride either," he reminded her. "This is how marriage arrangements are made sometimes. I am my brother's proxy. If I am trustworthy enough for him, then I should be trustworthy enough for you."

She looked away. "I know nothing about either of you."

"You'll learn all you need to in the days ahead. Now cease your stalling and prepare to leave this place for what you know can only be better."

Vivian knew she wasn't safe in Kilkerran any longer, and still she hesitated. "How do I know I can trust you?"

"Do you have any other option?" he asked, his voice clipped.

Before she knew what he was doing, he reached out and scooped her into his arms.

She cried out in protest.

He ignored her as he carried her farther into the room and tossed her on the bed. "There is no escape from your fate, Vivian. Tonight, it begins."

She scrambled away from him on the bed, never taking her eyes from his. "What begins?"

Quinn backed through the door. "We leave soon for Redhouse Castle in East Lothian." He sent her a long look. "You will be my brother's bride."

CHAPTER THREE

QUINN'S HAND TIGHTENED on the door latch as the color in Lady Vivian Campbell's cheeks deepened to a profound shade of pink. Perhaps he could have handled things a little more elegantly, but he had a mission to accomplish for both the king and his brother. He couldn't disappoint either of them.

With a tinderbox like her, his task would not be easy. Her fiery-red hair had given her identity away the moment his horse had nearly trampled her. The king had showed him a miniature that had been created while she'd been at court. The portrait had not captured the true nature of the unusual woman before him. In the image her features had been finely drawn. Reality, however, gave her full and tempting lips, lush lashes, and large, almond-shaped eyes that sparked with emotion.

"If you would stay safe, remain in this chamber." His heart thwacked against his rib cage as he took one last look at the storm that gathered in her blue eyes before he shut the door. Beautiful and headstrong. The woman would be a handful once he released her from this room. Quinn stalked down the long hallway and stopped at the head of the stairs. Below, his cousin Lachlan stood, waiting.

His cousin was a Douglas in every way Quinn was not. Lachlan's golden hair and bright blue eyes were a family trait shared by all except Quinn, whose dark hair and dark eyes always looked out of place. Even his brother, his blond twin, called him the black sheep of the Douglas clan. But that black sheep had saved his brother's life more than once in battle.

Reid was the fighter of the pair. Quinn was the peacemaker. Yet Reid's quest for excitement, for battle, had sent the two of them to war more often than not. It didn't seem to matter the cause, Reid was always ready to fight. At present, his brother was in pursuit of an enemy to the crown, Francis Stewart, the Earl of Bothwell, who had recently escaped from Edinburgh Castle, which was why Quinn was here with Vivian now. His brother had chosen to wage warfare over wooing his future wife.

Quinn only hoped that once Reid met the unusual woman who would be his bride that he'd settle down and become the leader the clan needed. The Douglas twins had been at war too long. If Quinn wanted to retire his sword, he needed his brother to finally take up his responsibility to the clan as the eldest son.

At Quinn's elongated silence, his cousin climbed the stairs and searched Quinn's face. "Is everything well?"

Quinn shook away his wayward thoughts. He had to stay

focused on his task. The morning's events had proven to him that none of them were safe in this village with Vivian in their care. Now that she was awake and the wound on her arm was bound, they had to leave as soon as possible. "Just planning our next move."

"What move is that?" Lachlan asked.

"For now, guard this door. Make sure Lady Campbell doesn't leave."

Lachlan hesitated, rubbing the back of his neck. "Is it safe?"

Quinn's brows came together. "What are you worried about? She's but a girl."

Lachlan bit his bottom lip before answering. "They called her a witch."

"She's no witch."

"How do you know?"

Quinn stepped closer to his cousin. "Because witches don't exist. Stop allowing the fears of others to influence you. Now guard the door."

With a look of chagrin, Lachlan nodded.

Quinn felt a moment's relief. Their journey would be that much more difficult if he had to fight Lachlan's fears and Vivian's resistance. Lachlan respected Quinn's authority and would do as he asked regardless of his own reservations. Vivian would be harder to control. He had hoped his brother's betrothed would simply accept her fate. Perhaps time to herself to consider her options would make her more receptive when he returned to fetch her. He had saved her from the angry crowd. The woman could show a little gratitude for his efforts. If only she would let him, he would whisk her away to safety again.

Quinn's gaze hardened on Lachlan. "I'll gather food and supplies while Moreis readies the horses. We'll send for you when we're set to leave. Until then, make sure she stays put."

"Understood," Lachlan replied before heading to the bedchamber door to stand guard.

Knowing he could trust Lachlan to do as he asked, Quinn took the stairs to the common room below. The lighting was dim. It took him a moment to find Moreis in the back of the room crowded with those gathering for an evening meal.

Quinn wove his way through the tables, assessing any vibrations of danger, and taking note of the men who watched him both blatantly and from the shadows. Often people were intimidated by his dark looks if not the sword at his side. In Kilkerran, he wasn't certain what to expect. The Campbells were an unpredictable bunch, or so the rumors claimed.

"Will she go with us willingly?" Moreis asked when Quinn took the seat opposite him. He continued to assess the room's occupants for malice.

"Probably not."

Moreis's mouth became a slash. "We've got more laudanum if things get out of hand."

"Let's leave drugging her as a last option. It's my hope she'll be more reasonable after she's had some time to think about her choices."

"Ye gave her choices?" Moreis said with disgust.

Quinn glared at his old friend. "I've known women like her—women who are isolated. They're hard to handle if they feel trapped."

Moreis snorted. "Since when are ye an expert on women?"

Quinn pushed his hands through his hair, ignoring the comment. "I know what's at stake here. Nothing might go wrong if we leave quickly. Gather the horses and wait for us behind the stable."

Moreis nodded, then stood. He understood the need for stealth. He'd also witnessed the villagers' reaction to Vivian.

Responding to the intense scrutiny of the men around him with his own mercurial gaze, Quinn stood. "Meet you shortly." He made his way back to the kitchen, willing to pay whatever was necessary for the supplies that would see them through the week-long journey ahead.

VIVIAN WAITED A few minutes after Quinn left before she quietly opened the bedchamber door. This time the long hallway wasn't empty. To the left of the door stood a young man with golden-blond hair, his posture erect. His gaze shifted toward her and he offered her a tight-lipped smile. The young man wasn't merely passing by her room. He was her guard.

Closing the door with a soft snap, Vivian looked futilely about the room for another means of escape. There wasn't one. The window was far too small for her to squeeze through. She blew out a breath and tried to come to terms with all that had happened to her in the last few hours. The situation had revealed her gift in a way that would no longer allow her to stay in Kilkerran. Her abductor had swept her away from a dangerous mob to relative safety. He'd drugged her, tended her wound, then threatened her with orders from the king to marry his brother. She knew nothing about her supposed betrothed. Yet that was hardly the worst of her problems at present.

Nay, her biggest problem was the man who had trapped her here. She'd never seen a man more powerfully male. It was more than his muscles, though they were impressive. There was something else that fed into the indomitable male aura that clung to him. One that spelled danger for anyone foolish enough to cross him.

And yet cross him she would. She would not submit to another marriage any more than she would give herself over to those who had labeled her a witch. Nerves jangling, mind reeling, she crossed the room to the window and threw the shutter open. Lifting her face to the cold wind, she let the evening chill chase the frightening thoughts from her mind.

Her gaze focused on the world beyond the inn yard below. There were dangers out there, she knew. She'd been fighting those dangers since she'd started having visions as a young child.

She'd be a fool to turn away Quinn's help. He was strong enough to go up against her greatest threat: Rupert, the man who wanted to destroy her and anyone else who was different.

There really was no other choice but to leave with Quinn and his men. Perhaps in time she could convince him to take her to Inishail Convent instead of to his brother. There she could figure out a way out of the betrothal contract. The king was not unsympathetic to her. She might be able to convince him to nullify the contract for Reid Douglas's sake and her own during these difficult times. She could stay at the convent until either the "witch fever" ended or everyone, including Rupert, forgot about her. Only then could she embrace the life she'd always wanted for herself—to find a cottage in a distant village where she could live alone and heal those who were sick or injured without the fear of being persecuted.

Free of the bonds of marriage and motherhood, she would be content. Happy even. She had the funds she needed to support her dream since she'd saved all the tokens her patients had given her over the years. In doing so, she'd amassed a small portable inheritance of her own, hidden away in the last place anyone would look for such a thing.

Her gaze drifted to the hem of her gown as she released a tired sigh. Clinging to her dream, Vivian shut the window and moved back to the bed to wait for Quinn to take her from this place. She was ready to cooperate for now.

She didn't have to wait long. She had barely settled on the bed when a knock came at the door.

"Are you ready to travel?" Quinn asked, entering the room. He picked up her cloak and offered it to her.

She accepted the garment, draping it around her shoulders then pulling the hood up over her hair. "It seems leaving with you is my only option."

His eyes narrowed. "The more cooperative you are, the easier this will be. We are not out of danger yet."

She nodded. "I understand the dangers."

"If you don't, you soon will," he said, turning his back to her and heading out the door. "Follow me."

He led her out the back door of the inn and through the darkness toward the stable. If he was surprised by her sudden compliance with his plans he didn't show it. His face grim, he approached two other men already on horseback and a third black stallion.

"Milady." Quinn's gaze connected with hers. "Meet your traveling companions: Moreis MacMinrie and Lachlan Douglas." Quinn motioned to the older man first then the younger who'd been her guard abovestairs.

"A pleasure," she replied without thinking. What lay ahead of them would be anything but pleasant if the swords at their hips and the targes on their backs were any indication. They were expecting trouble.

"Let's go," Quinn prompted.

"Where's my horse?" Vivian asked.

"You're riding with me," Quinn said an instant before he swung up onto the saddle of his big black horse. He offered her his arm, and when she clasped it, he hauled her up and settled her in front of him. Instantly his warmth and the scent of cloves enveloped her. She tried to sit forward, to avoid any kind of contact, but that was impossible as the spurred horse launched into a steady rhythm.

The night was crisp and a first quarter moon hung overhead, casting everything around them in dappled, silver light. Except for the sound of hoofbeats against the packed earth, silence surrounded them. The man at her back was quiet, extending her no polite chatter.

Her eyes darted, taking in their direction, the familiar path toward the outskirts of the village and the rocky terrain beyond. They were heading for the other side of the peninsula.

When she could take the silence no longer she asked the question that pounded in her thoughts with every step they took from Kilkerran: "If the betrothal of myself to your brother is true, then why did *you* come to get me?" Vivian frowned into the darkness. "Taking me to your brother will be no easy feat. What are you to gain from all of this? Fortune? Fame? There must be something."

"I apologize for my bluntness back at the inn. You were questioning things I have no control over either. Reid asked me to retrieve you, so I came."

"You always do what your brother asks?"

Quinn's muscles tightened against her back. "Reid is my elder brother and leader of our clan. It is my duty to do as he asks."

"Why?"

"Because I want him to be happy."

She twisted toward him. "You think I will make him happy? You don't even know me. And what you have learned so far should scare you more than comfort you."

He leaned close. "Reid will be a fine laird. You will be as happy with him as he is with you."

"Just what I awoke today dreaming of," she countered.

He grinned, then his features became thoughtful. "All right, Lady Campbell. If not marriage, then what do you truly dream of?"

"I shall not tell you that," she said, turning back around.

"Why not? We are to be related eventually. You need not have secrets from me."

She straightened. "You tell me something about yourself first. What do you dream of besides cavorting across the country doing your brother's bidding?"

He laughed, the sound rich and warm. "You're a spirited one. Reid will like that. All right, you wish to know my dreams? I'll tell you one. It is my hope that when Reid settles down I can pursue a long-held dream to make my living from the earth."

"You wish to be a farmer?"

He shrugged. "I wish for peace and tranquility. The land has always provided me with that."

His response was not what she expected. "I hope your dream becomes a real—" Vivian broke off at the sound of a bush rustling. She tensed.

Quinn leaned forward and whispered close to her ear. "It's only the wind."

But she knew it wasn't. She closed her eyes, her lips forming a silent prayer as pain assailed her temples and a vision flashed across her mind.

Six men on horseback with torches burning bright against the blackness of night, waiting behind the rocks. Six swords at the ready. The glint of a narrowed eye.

Blood drummed in her temples. Her heart pounded painfully as she leaned back into the solid firmness of Quinn's chest. "Stop the horses." Her whispered words cut through the night. She drew in a deep breath, trying to hold back the nausea that always followed her visions.

The beast beneath them came to a halt along with the others. "What is it?" Quinn asked. Lachlan and Moreis stopped beside them.

Even though Quinn had saved her life and had not been frightened when the villagers had called her a witch, she wasn't ready to tell him about her gift. Yet she had to warn him of the danger ahead. The darkness pressed in on her as she trained her eyes ahead, searching for a sign that the men were truly there. And then she saw it, a faint reddish-orange tinge above the rocks. "There." She pointed into the distance. "Fire, perhaps torches, and a possible ambush ahead."

No sooner had she spoken the words than shouts and the sound of hoofbeats broke the silence. Vivian's heart lurched as she clutched her fingers around the leather saddle before her. Six riders, torches blazing, came at them. No doubt because of her escape from Kilkerran Castle Rupert had put a bounty on her head. He would turn the entire country against her, paying anyone to bring her back to him, dead or alive.

A chill slid through Vivian when the six riders reined to a halt nearby; two of the men were in the act of dismounting. A swift impression of them revealed fierce expressions, made even more so by the flickering flames of the torches. A third man dismounted and stepped toward them. His eyes were small and ferret-like, and when they flicked over Vivian she was hard-pressed to restrain a shudder of revulsion.

"Hand over the witch tae be burned and we'll let ye leave peacefully," the third burly man growled as he threw his torch to the ground and drew his sword.

"You know this man?" Quinn asked Vivian.

"Nay," she replied, not recognizing any of the three who had revealed themselves. They were unshaven and unwashed. Their tunics were crusted with filth, their hair shiny with grease, and their hands blackened by the soot from the torches. Whispers passed between the men still on horseback.

Behind her, she could feel Quinn's muscles tighten. He reached for his boot. In a blur of motion, he flung a dagger into the chest of the third man. The brute fell backward just as the other five men advanced, three on horseback, two on foot, swords drawn. Their angry cries echoed in the night, sending shivers across Vivian's chilled flesh.

Quinn lifted Vivian from his horse, propelling her toward a cluster of bushes off to the left with such force that she stumbled and fell. "Stay back." He drew his sword and advanced, shouting an order to Moreis and Lachlan to attack.

Vivian's breath caught as one of the men on horseback charged Quinn. The broadsword came slashing in an arc toward Quinn's torso, but his sword came down to block the strike. The biting sound of steel on steel rang in the air, punctuating the crackle and roar of the flames from the torches now abandoned in the dirt.

Mounted, Moreis and Lachlan leapt into battle, quickly taking down the two other men on horseback, then charging the two men on foot.

Quinn fixed his attention on his own adversary with a calm, steady gaze. He was so intent on the conflict he didn't notice the man he had stopped with his dagger had regained his feet. The man pulled the weapon from his chest, then pointed it toward Vivian as he came closer, his own blood running down his chin. "This will end here and now, Witch."

"I'm no witch. I'm a healer," Vivian protested as she shuffled back, searching the ground for a rock or a stick, anything with which to defend herself.

The man forced a gurgling laugh as he strode toward her, his weapon trained on her, his wounded body tense. "I've seen yer magic with my own eyes."

"Saving a boy's life is not magic." Fear gripped her as a contorted smile came to his lips. She clutched the end of a stick.

Metal flashed in the ghostly moonlight as the man lunged for her chest. Vivian blocked the thrust with her stick. The wood quivered before it split in two, leaving her defenseless once more.

She braced herself, ready to fight him with her hands, as he came at her again. The anger on his face told her he wouldn't stop until he killed her. He raised the dagger, ready to strike, then he stopped abruptly. A red, grotesque blossom of blood spread across his chest. In the next instant, he fell forward, landing at her feet.

Vivian cried out and leapt back at the sight of a sword thrust through the man's back. Then Quinn was there, lifting her in his arms, holding her tight as he moved back to his horse.

"Are you unharmed?" He searched her face. When she didn't answer, he set her down and brought a hand up to brush a wayward strand of hair from her cheek.

She nodded, not trusting her voice. She stared up at him, tempted to rest her head on his chest until she saw a rivulet of blood coming from his temple. "You're hurt."

"I'm well enough." He stiffened and dropped his hand to his side. "I know you're shaken, but we must keep moving. The farther we get from this village, the safer we'll all be."

"Agreed." She *was* shaken. If it hadn't been for Quinn and his men, she would be dead. How had she ever allowed herself to believe she could escape Rupert on her own?

Vivian clutched her hands together to keep them from trembling as Quinn settled her on his horse. Moreis and Lachlan were mounted and ready as he left her side to return to her attacker. Quinn retrieved his dagger and his sword, and after wiping the blades he returned them to his boot and scabbard. Once those tasks were complete, he mounted behind her.

"A change of plans," Quinn said to Moreis and Lachlan with irritation. "We must now thread our way north, through the Grampian Mountains. With luck, we'll avoid anyone else who thinks we are still heading for the peninsula and the quickest route back to the mainland."

Both men agreed and they started forward once more, moving silently through the night. They hadn't gone far when a shadow separated itself from the darkness.

CHAPTER FOUR

VIVIAN TENSED. THIS intruder hadn't been part of her vision. The rider on horseback moved into their path. Quinn's arms tightened around Vivian.

In a fluid motion, Quinn transferred the reins to one hand and drew his sword. "Lean down against the horse's mane and hold tight," he said next to Vivian's cheek. "No matter what happens, don't let go."

Her heartbeat pulsing in her ears Vivian did as instructed, holding the horse tightly. She could feel the flexing of the beast's muscles beneath her body as the three of them jolted forward.

"Halt!" a shriek split through the air. "I'm nae yer enemy!"

Vivian sat upright, recognizing the voice. "Gillis?"

"Aye, m'lady." The older woman's response quivered with fear.

Vivian twisted around to meet Quinn's puzzled gaze. "She is my maid and no threat to us."

He drew back on the reins, stopping his horse.

"What now?" Moreis's tone was exasperated as he and

Lachlan stopped.

The tension left Quinn's body though he did not sheathe his weapon as the rider approached.

A sense of relief washed through Vivian as Gillis came into sight. "What are you doing here? You should have stayed at the castle."

The maid's stark-white hair nearly glowed beneath the light of the moon. Her face wore a heavy look of concern. "I could do nae such thing. Not when I knew ye were in trouble." The old woman's features suddenly filled with suspicion and her gaze narrowed on Quinn and his men. "Are ye well, m'lady? Should I raise the alarm?"

"Nay!" Vivian replied. The last thing they needed was more unwanted attention headed their way. "These men helped me."

Gillis did not look convinced as she urged her horse to move closer. "I'm here to help ye as well." She reached behind her saddle.

Quinn tensed. His sword inched upward.

Vivian put her hand on his arm, stalling further actions. "It's all right. Gillis would never harm me or any of you."

Quinn stared down at her hand.

Vivian pulled her fingers away.

"I'll judge who is and who is not a threat for myself," he said, his tone harsh as he continued to assess her maid.

"I know ye had tae leave the castle in a hurry this mornin'." Gillis drew out a bundle wrapped in a blanket. "I brought ye yer favorite gown and a few other things I could sneak out without causin' alarm."

"That was kind of you, Gillis," Vivian said, meaning the words. The two of them had only known each other for the last six months, and yet the woman had become a dear friend to Vivian during her amicable, but passionless marriage.

"How did you know where to find us?" Quinn pressed the older woman.

"'Tis my duty tae follow milady wherever she goes. I've been near her side ever since she arrived at Kilkerran Castle, even without her knowin' it." Gillis's expression steeled. "I followed her into the village this mornin', tae the coachin' inn, then here. While ye fought with the others, I circled around tae be in front of ye, to challenge ye if the need arose."

Quinn arched a brow. "With no weapon?"

Gillis sat taller on her horse. "A woman needs nae weapon tae dare tae protect what she loves."

Quinn continued to assess the maid for a long moment before he finally sheathed his sword. He maneuvered his horse alongside the maid's and accepted the bundle. "You took a great risk coming here. Anyone could have followed you."

"Nay," Gillis protested. "I was careful."

"Thank you again, Gillis," Vivian replied. "You've risked enough. You must return to the castle before you are missed. I could not live with myself if something happened to you."

"Return?" Gillis shook her ghostly white head. "Nay, m'lady. 'Tis my duty tae go with ye. Wherever ye go, that is my place."

Vivian startled. She'd no idea the woman had taken her duty so deeply to heart. Then just as quickly wild despair tore through her. If Gillis had been that close to her, what had she witnessed?

"Nay," Quinn objected. "We'll be traveling fast. My men and I will see your mistress to safety from here."

Gillis's lips set stubbornly. "It's nae proper fer three men tae be travelin' with a woman alone. I'll be right beside her tae protect her from all of ye. Don't deny it. 'Tis only right fer me tae come along."

Behind her, Vivian could feel the tension return to Quinn's chest and thighs. That tension flowed into Vivian, adding to her own anxiety. Did Gillis know about her visions? And, miraculously, felt obligated to Vivian anyway?

The older woman had been truly faithful to her since her arrival at Kilkerran. Why did Vivian suddenly fear what Gillis might reveal about her gift? Adding to the complexity of the situation was the sudden realization that Gillis's life could also be in danger. If the villagers believed Vivian to be a witch they might also accuse Gillis of being one.

Moreis nodded. "The woman has a point," he said with a smile that showed a gap in his lower teeth.

Quinn released a tired sigh. "I'll leave the decision to your mistress."

His deferral caught Vivian off guard as her gaze passed between Quinn and her maid. "Gillis travels with us." There was no other choice if Vivian wanted to make certain her maid did not end up tried as a witch.

"So be it." The words were tight. Quinn signaled to Moreis and Lachlan to take position behind the older woman. To Gillis he said, "Prepare for a hard ride. We must make haste if we're not to find ourselves in the middle of more unwanted attention."

The raw edge to his voice brought Vivian's gaze back to his. He stared at her with an intensity that made her understand—possibly for the first time—just how determined Quinn was to see her delivered to his brother.

"You can stop looking at me like I'm some kind of ogre. I'm not going to hurt you."

"You've changed your mind about forcing me to marry your brother then?" she challenged.

A flicker of agitation crossed his brow. "You will do your duty just as I will do mine," he said over her head as he kicked their horse into a gallop.

Her breath caught as the sudden movement sent the wind rushing around them, snatching her hair and freeing the long tresses. Quinn and Vivian flew along an untried path with only the moon to guide them through the dark mottled shadows. Their speed swept away all sound as the stallion soared over an outcrop of rocks that lay across their path, then came to earth again.

The very air seemed to hang in breathless suspense as an eerie mist formed close to the ground. They would make it safely through the night. No sooner had she released the thought that was part prayer and part plea when a telltale pain flashed across her temples and an image formed in her mind's eye.

She was in a cave, or a shelter of some sort. There the ever-changing brilliance of a small fire. Quinn stretched out on a blanket. She sensed every action of his body: the rise and fall of his chest as he breathed. The tension in his hand as it gripped the blanket. The slight hollow beneath the bones of his cheeks as his lips tightened. And his eyes . . . they looked at her with desire.

The scent of rain. Earth. Burning wood; the scents surrounded them. She wanted to breathe in the aroma, and his scents, to gather them inside her senses, to remember them forever.

She closed her eyes. She opened them just as quickly as her vision changed.

Fire. Dry timber below her feet. Flames, licking hungrily toward the sky. Heat. She struggled against restraints. A laugh that blended with the chanting all around her. "Burn the witch, burn the witch."

A crowd. The roar of the flames. Choking gray smoke. Fear. Anger. Pain. Despair, then weariness as the flames took hold.

A voice drifted to her as if through a long tunnel, reaching her with blurred and muted words, entreating her to respond. "Lady Campbell, can you hear me?" The murmured inquiry increased in volume. "Milady, what's wrong?"

She gasped for breath even as her stomach lurched. Vivian clamped her mouth shut and swallowed convulsively. Her nerves jangling, her mind reeling, she blinked until the indistinct shadow resolved into an image of Quinn. Her muscles weak, she slumped to one side despite the ice-cold fear cascading through her.

Quinn held her in his arms atop his horse. They'd stopped moving. Confusion was etched deeply on his face. "What happened? You were here, but you weren't."

Her heart thundered in her chest. She'd had not one, but two visions in a row thanks to the laudanum they'd given her. All her life she had tried not to be terrified by what she saw. The pleasant images, like the moment shared between herself and Quinn, she could possibly manipulate in a way that was more to her liking. Such as on this journey they might enter a cave, but that did not mean she had to give in to the more sensual parts of what she had seen. The second vision of her burning at the stake would be far more difficult to avoid.

She'd tried to change a vision before, once partially and once from beginning to end. The former had ended in success, the latter in devastation.

Vivian drew a careful breath, then another, as she pulled herself back from her visions. A long moment ticked past until she felt more in control.

"Are you well?" Quinn asked. The words were heavy

with doubt.

She looked up into his expressive face and nodded. She ran a dry tongue over her parched lips. "I'm so tired. I must have fallen into a dream," she lied, pressing her trembling fingers to her aching temples. She'd been warned by others as well as the king to never reveal her visions, but she'd never seen her own death before. The images of what-could-be flashed through her mind once more. She flinched at the memory then forced herself to be still, to silence the fear rushing through her.

Quinn studied her, his eyes searching, the strength of his gaze holding her immobile. Dark eyes, not so unlike those in her vision, looked at her now with concern and suspicion. "Whatever it is . . . you can tell me."

It would be so easy to trust him. To think she could open herself to another and tell him about her gift. Then she wouldn't have to stand alone against whatever the future brought her way. Her hands itched to reach out and touch him, to find a semblance of comfort in this man as she had in the first part of her vision.

As if proving the path toward her first vision had already begun, he reached up and caressed her cheek. "Let me help, Lady Campbell."

"Please, call me Vivian." An overwhelming rush of heat sliced from his body into hers. She trembled at the force of it. She drew in a sharp breath and pulled free of his touch. There was nothing between them. There never could be.

Perhaps that was the answer, and why she'd had both visions on top of each other. If she kept herself apart from Quinn Douglas so as to avert the first vision, then it stood to reason that the second vision might not come to pass.

Vivian clenched her teeth. Avoiding her visions had never worked for her in the past. Why did she think such a thing would help her now? It hadn't helped Sister Emmelia escape a disastrous fate.

But if Vivian were careful, if she paid attention to the signs, then at least she would have forewarning of the events as they unfolded. And, in time, she could find a way to shape them to her benefit. Until then, she needed Quinn's protection. She would never survive without it. Quinn's gaze had been measuring her while her thoughts churned. The look in his eyes said he wanted to press her for more of an explanation, but instead on a sigh of exasperation he said, "If that is all you have to say on the subject, then let us delay no longer. The farther we are from Rupert Campbell and his men, the better for us all."

CHAPTER FIVE

A S THE FIVE travelers continued their journey, the deep purple fingers of dawn gave way to brighter skies. The warming rays of the morning sunshine pushed the chill of the night away, reawakening Quinn's senses. At the realization, he finally slowed his horse's pace. They'd reached the edge of the forest just outside of Tarbert.

They were still in Campbell territory and needed to hurry to a safer locale. Vivian had fallen asleep in his arms a few hours ago. Gillis had almost tumbled from her horse twice in the last hour. Moreis and Lachlan had not complained, but Quinn could see the telltale signs of weariness in both of their faces.

Quinn continued on until the party was deeper into the forest and sheltered by the trees before he brought his horse to a halt. Exhaustion had settled into the marrow of his bones. With each passing moment, it grew harder to keep his senses alert for signs of danger. And, if the quivering of Odin's muscles beneath his legs were any indication, his horse needed a break every bit as much as the rest of them. "We'll stop here for a few hours."

"Praise the heavens!" Moreis grumbled, sliding from his horse's back only to groan all the louder as he stretched his stiff muscles.

Lachlan rolled his eyes at the older man. "We'll prepare the sleeping rolls," Quinn's cousin said as he dismounted. Together, the two of them removed the heavy packs from their horses' backs, preparing to make camp.

Gillis collapsed against her horse's neck. "I've nae strength left tae get off this beast."

As though his muscles no longer ached, Moreis hurried to the older woman's side and carefully lifted her from the saddle. He settled her at the base of a nearby tree. "Rest here, while we arrange a blanket fer ye."

Gillis yawned. "I should see tae m'lady."

"No need," Quinn said, handing a still-sleeping Vivian into Lachlan's arms for a moment before he dismounted and took her back into his own.

Vivian's eyes fluttered open. "Where are we?"

"A brief stop. Go back to sleep," Quinn said softly.

With a sigh, she nestled deeper into his arms and closed her eyes once more.

Moreis settled a blanket on the ground near Gillis and signaled to Quinn. "Place the girl here." To Gillis he said, "Watch over yer ladyship if ye must, but ye both need sleep. We'll be here fer a few hours. Then we have another day of hard riding ahead."

Gillis nodded and scooted closer to Vivian, sharing the

blanket Moreis set down. No sooner had she stopped moving than her eyes drifted shut and her breathing became slow and even.

Moreis released a chuckle. "Guess that means I'll be lookin' after her horse. I can take the first watch as well."

Quinn led his horse over to the others. He tethered Odin to the lower branches of a tree, giving the animal enough lead to graze. "I'll care for all the horses and keep watch. You both get some sleep."

"Bless ye, lad," Moreis said with a grateful grin before settling atop a blanket not far from the women.

"What about you?" Lachlan frowned. "You're as tired as the rest of us."

Quinn gave him a brief smile. It was just like Lachlan to be concerned about everyone else's welfare. "Can I wake you in a couple of hours to relieve me?"

"Agreed," the younger man said before turning away to settle atop his own woolen blanket. Within minutes the sounds of slow, even breathing filled the makeshift camp.

After securing the horses and removing their saddles, Quinn rubbed the tired beasts down. He rummaged through his pack and removed a parcel of oats he'd brought with him and offered each of the horses a handful. To Odin he gave a slightly bigger portion. His horse was larger and had carried a heavier load. Odin nudged him with his muzzle.

Quinn chuckled as he rubbed the beast's neck. "You're welcome." His amusement was short-lived as thoughts of water entered his mind. The horses needed refreshment and the flasks needed refilling. There had to be a creek around somewhere.

They seemed to have outdistanced for now any of the villagers from Kilkerran who might still pursue them. But they had to stay vigilant. As word spread about what had happened in Kilkerran, others would come for them and the bounty someone had obviously offered for Vivian's return.

Indecisive about what he should risk, Quinn tossed a quick glance back over the camp. Everyone slept, including Vivian. He should stay close and make certain they were protected, yet they desperately needed water. Perhaps if he only scouted the area within eyeshot he could still protect them all while finding a source of water.

Set on a course of action, Quinn headed to the west, deeper into the forest. Weak sunlight filtered through the tree boughs overhead, lighting his path. The only sounds that greeted him were those of the birds twittering above and his own footfalls on the verdant blanket of moss that covered the forest floor.

He turned to check his distance. He could still see the camp and four supine bodies. Since everything was as it should be, he continued on, this time heading north. He hadn't gone ten paces when he heard the trickling sound of a stream. Four more paces and he saw the shimmer of water reflecting the weak sunlight.

Breathing a satisfied sigh, Quinn turned back toward

camp, eager to bring the horses to this location for a well-deserved respite. He nodded with satisfaction and despite his exhaustion moved forward. He once again surveyed the camp and then did a double take. There were only three bodies lying on the ground. Four horses still remained tethered to the trees.

Vivian was nowhere in sight.

VIVIAN'S EYES FLICKERED open. Her first thought was that she could no longer feel the horse swaying beneath her or feel Quinn's warmth wrapped around her. She'd felt secure enough in his arms to fall into a deep sleep. That had never happened to her before with any man.

Sitting up, she cast a glance around. She saw Gillis nestled beside her, asleep. Only a few yards away lay Moreis and Lachlan. But where was Quinn? She stood and stretched the ache that had settled in her lower back as she looked about the campsite. He was nowhere to be seen. Should she be worried?

All four of their horses were still tethered to the bushes nearby. The animals rustled the low branches in search of fresh blades of grass hidden beneath. The giant beast she and Quinn had ridden did not look alarmed at the absence of his master so why should she be? Quinn was most likely scouting the area, searching for water or other supplies to help them on their journey.

At the thought the tension in her shoulders eased, though it didn't disappear. She was grateful to Quinn for his help in the village, but they were far from safe while they were out in the open like this. And then there was the injury Quinn had sustained to his head during their escape. He'd refused her assistance earlier, but a wound like that could become putrid over time. Perhaps she should have a look around the area just to make certain he was well and had not succumbed to a fever or worse.

Vivian looked to the others who were sleeping nearby. She should wake one of them to come with her in her search. Heading for Moreis's bedroll, she bent down and shook his shoulder. "Moreis?"

His response was a loud snore.

With a frown, she moved on to Quinn's cousin. "Lachlan, please wake up. I need your help."

He did not respond at all.

Her frown deepened as she moved beside her sleeping maid. "Gillis?"

The older woman slept soundly, and Vivian knew she'd find no help there. The whole group had been pushed to exhaustion and they were reaping the benefit of sleep now.

With a sigh Vivian turned back toward the forest. Going off on her own would be dangerous, but she would never forgive herself if something happened to Quinn when she had the skills to prevent it. Leaving the camp behind, Vivian stepped carefully across the forest floor riddled with overgrown roots. "Quinn, where are you?" she called, searching the area. He wouldn't have gone far.

Determined to find him and make certain he was all right, she made her way through the underbrush. Low-hung branches snagged her skirt and snatched at her hair as she continued toward what appeared to be a stream. At the edge of the glistening water she bent down and, cupping her hands, brought a measure of the cool liquid to her lips. In the next moment, a huge pair of hands caught her under her arms and hauled her off her feet. "Quinn?"

"'Fraid not," an unfamiliar voice growled behind her. Male arms tightened around her.

Vivian screamed and lashed out, managing to land a solid blow to her attacker's jaw. Without hesitation he struck back, bringing his fist up to catch her solidly in the chin. Her head snapped back, her teeth rattled, and pain radiated through her jaw, stunning her. Even so, she kicked out wildly in a blind attempt to free herself. She heard a grunt of pain.

"Tie the witch up," a female voice said.

"I'm trying." Another man grabbed her ankles and attempted to hold her still while the first man tightened his hold. Vivian bucked in their grasp, writhing and struggling, but they were too strong.

"Hurry! The others will have heard her scream," the woman said.

"The witch won't get away this time," the man who held her whispered against her ear, his tone threatening, while the other man tied her hands before her with a length of rope.

An icy shiver slithered down Vivian's spine. Her attackers had been following them all along, merely waiting until Vivian separated herself from the others to move in . . . and now she was caught, trapped.

"Yer stupidity is our good fortune. Among the others we couldna touch ye," the man holding her said as he let go.

Bound at the arms and feet, she teetered and slammed against the ground. She clenched her teeth as pain radiated through her injured arm. Shifting to her back, Vivian got her first clear look at her attackers. The taller man she recognized as Clifton Lorne, a mason whom she'd met at Kilkerran Castle last week when she'd bandaged a deep cut on his hand.

Beside him and staring down at her with disdain were the weaver, William Abbott, and his wife, Maura. William had been the one in the village who'd called her a witch. "Why are you doing this?" Vivian asked. "I helped to heal your son. Does my saving the child's life mean nothing to you?"

William's face reddened. "Nae, this is because I fear what ye did to him, ye being a witch and all."

"I'm not a witch," Vivian objected, desperate to somehow reason with her captors. She'd known and helped these people over the past months. "I'm a healer, nothing more."

Her only hope was to convince them she was innocent.

Clifton grasped her head and tied a gag across her mouth, silencing her. "Yer innocence or guilt is nae fer us tae decide. All we want is the bounty we'll get fer capturing ye."

"We've earned our reward fer followin' ye all night." William's eyes were bright with both fear and excitement.

No doubt Rupert was responsible for the bounty. It would make their journey even more perilous if she somehow managed to escape her current predicament.

Maura stood beside her husband and watched Vivian warily. "Can she hurt us on the way back tae Kilkerran?"

"Nae when she's trussed up like a pig goin' tae slaughter." Clifton laughed as he booted her in the ribs.

Vivian's cry of pain was muted by her gag. The truth didn't matter to her captors. Only how much they could gain. She wished she had remained with the others back in the safety of the campsite. Alone and in the open, she had no protection.

Witches had no rights, not even the bishop's clause—a test once offered to witches to prove their innocence if they could read a passage from the Bible—could protect her now. Vivian swallowed past the ache in her throat. People didn't care what happened to those accused of witchcraft. Since King James's proclamation to find and destroy all witches went out shortly after he had sent her to Dugald Campbell, all it took was an innuendo, a rumor, or an enemy with a grudge, and anyone could find themselves taken to a tribunal with no hope of release.

Vivian looked up into Clifton's face. His features and jaw could have been carved in the limestone he chiseled every day. His eyes were filled with greed. As Clifton bent down and lifted her from the ground, then threw her over his shoulder like a sack of grain, Vivian's muted scream called out to the one man who could have saved her from this fate.

Quinn Douglas.

CHAPTER SIX

H E'D HEARD HER scream. Knowing time was of the essence, Quinn raced back to Odin. Then, giving a shout to the others to wake them, he rushed after Vivian.

Quinn forced a sudden and unexpected turmoil inside him aside as he studied the soil on the northern side of the stream. There had been a struggle. Vivian had been forced to the ground by two men and a woman if he were reading the footprints they'd left behind correctly. Three captors. If only he could determine where they'd taken Vivian, he would willingly battle the others for her safe return.

Mounting his horse, Quinn followed the trail. Vivian's attackers were on horseback as well. Their path led from the edge of the forest back out into the open as though they no longer feared discovery.

Why had Vivian risked capture by leaving the camp? Why had he not stayed to make certain she was safe? Quinn frowned. There would be plenty of time to blame himself over that mistake later. For now, he had to find his brother's soon-to-be wife and keep her alive.

Quinn's body tensed and his hands curled around the

leather reins. At a nicker of displeasure from Odin, he relaxed his grip, focusing on the trail of tamped-down moss and hoofprints his newly made enemies had left behind.

What if they'd killed her already? Even as the thought materialized, Quinn rejected it. Whoever had taken Vivian had been following them. They hadn't attacked like the first group of villagers who were scared by what they thought Vivian was or what she could do to them. Her captors wanted something from either Vivian or, through her, someone else. And they needed her alive to get that.

Taking comfort in the thought, Quinn pressed on. His thoughts turned to his brother. Quinn had left Redhouse Castle with the greatest of intentions: to bring Reid a wife with the hopes it would stop his brother's constant pursuit of danger. Yet, even Quinn knew the likelihood of Reid settling down was slim. Reid liked to live life on the edge, and for years Quinn had allowed his brother to pull him along on that quest. But Quinn was growing weary of constant warring and always watching his back.

He wanted peace. He wanted a family. He wanted to settle down with a woman whom he could cherish, and who would cherish him in return.

With someone like Vivian.

Quinn startled at the thought. Nay, he must not allow his thoughts to go there, for she was his brother's reward, not his. Despite having fought every battle beside his brother, shielding him from harm more often than not, Reid was the eldest and the first of them to pledge his loyalty to the king as one of his elite guards.

King James rewarded loyalty. Perhaps there would yet be some benefit that might come Quinn's way after Vivian was delivered safe and unharmed to her betrothed. If he could choose his own reward, it would be to finally attain the peace and serenity he longed for, away from fighting, away from war.

Quinn had been riding hard for several miles when a sight in the distance caught his eye. A splash of red hair highlighted by the morning sun. He dug his heels into Odin's sides. The horse responded with a surge of power. As man and horse rounded a bend, he again spotted Vivian, her hair flying like a banner in the wind.

A thrill moved through him that he had found her. At the pressure of his master's heels, Odin lowered his head and flew across the distance. Quinn knew he had to eliminate the rider who carried Vivian in front of him before engaging the others. It was the only way to ensure her safety since she was in no position to defend herself, bound as she was at the hands and feet.

He caught up to the riders. Hearing his approach, the three attackers turned, swords drawn. Outnumbered, Quinn knew he had to even the odds quickly. The man carrying Vivian on his horse roared like an enraged bull and launched forward, his sword clutched purposefully in his fist. The second man charged at the same moment.

Quinn plunged toward Vivian's captor.

Her eyes wild in her pale face, Vivian leaned forward against the horse's mane, clearing the way for Quinn's attack. With a stroke of his broadsword Quinn took her attacker's head clean off.

The terrified horse squealed as the body fell off, and shot forward with Vivian on its back. In that same instant, the second attacker's sword came at Quinn. Trying to avoid the lethal blade, Quinn hunched over Odin's neck, but too late. The edge caught the tip of his shoulder, slicing through his shirt to the flesh beneath.

As the man flew past, Quinn gathered his strength and struck him from behind with the flat of his sword, knocking the man to the ground, where he stayed in a heap.

"The witch is ours!" the female screamed as she chased the horse carrying Vivian away.

Not wanting to injure the woman, but needing to put her in her place, Quinn rode up beside her and plucked her from her horse's back, dumping her on the ground. He reined Odin to a stop. "That's enough."

"Who the hell are ye tae interfere?" the woman sputtered as her face contorted in a snarl. "We're carryin' out our duty."

Quinn locked his gaze with hers. "There is no duty to kill innocent people."

Her face empurpled. "She's a witch!"

"Leave."

Her ferret eyes widened. "M'laird will hear about this!"

"Leave. Now." Anger pulsed in Quinn's veins as he clenched the hilt of his sword.

As though finally realizing the extent of his anger, the woman scrambled back toward the second fallen man. He groaned as he tried to rise, only to collapse back against the dirt.

Quinn seized the moment and turned Odin in the direction of Vivian's panicked horse. As the two of them came alongside the frightened beast, he seized the horse's reins.

Odin flinched at the smell of blood, but he remained steady as Quinn stopped alongside Vivian's horse. Her fingers were tangled in the horse's mane. That was how she'd managed to stay atop the animal.

Relief pulsed through Quinn at the sight of Vivian's chest moving in and out. She was alive. A spray of blood covered the back of her cloak, but he was certain it was from her attacker and not her own.

Untangling her fingers, she reached for him with her bound hands.

Sheathing his sword, Quinn swept her onto Odin's back and into his arms. The moment she was free of the horse, the frightened beast bolted into the forest. Regretting the loss of the animal but needing to attend to Vivian more, Quinn decided not to chase the horse down. Instead, he retrieved his dagger from his boot and sliced through the cords at Vivian's hands and feet before untying her gag.

"Quinn!" She threw her arms around him and buried her face in the curve of his neck.

"Are you unharmed?" He hesitated for only a moment before he unfastened her cloak, tossed the bloody garment to the ground, then closed his arms tightly around her, as if he could absorb her suffering. He had no right to comfort his brother's bride so closely, but his arms remained around her. Where was his will? His reason? But reason too easily gave way under her needs as violent trembling racked her body. "You're safe," he whispered against her hair.

She hugged him harder.

For a long moment they remained that way, wrapped in each other's arms, until her trembling slowed. Eventually, she drew back, looking up into his eyes with regret. "I was a fool to leave the camp alone. When I couldn't find you—"

"Neither of us will make that mistake again." Her magnificent blue eyes still held fear, but also hope. With his thumb he stroked a droplet of blood from her chin, then her lower lip, rubbing lightly against the inviting fullness. When he realized what he was doing, he pulled back. "We should go. The others will be worried."

Vivian drew a shuddering breath and dropped her gaze to his shoulder. She tensed. "You're hurt." She reached for him.

"'Tis only a superficial wound, I am sure." He flinched away from her touch. His nerves were too raw for her to touch him with any kind of tenderness. She was to be his brother's wife. He'd best remember that. "We need to get back to the others."

Hurt reflected in her eyes for a heartbeat before it was replaced with pride. Her face was framed by a halo of red hair tossing in the relentless breeze. Fragility and strength, pride and iron resolve. He was seeing that the two of them were so different and yet so much alike. "Are you ready to return?" he asked this time instead of demanding.

His words pulled Vivian from the strange spell that had seemed to enclose them. "I'm ready."

Still holding her in his arms, he set Odin into a steady pace. When they passed two bodies on the path heading back toward their campsite, Vivian did not look away.

"They betrayed me for the bounty they could get."

Pain and uncertainty were etched clearly upon her bold features, and he longed to reassure her that as long as she stayed with him nothing would ever harm her again.

"Why are you helping me? You could have been killed. You still might before our journey is through. Wouldn't it be better for all of you to leave me someplace? Inishail Convent isn't far from here. The abbess is a friend."

There it was again—that look in her eyes: strength mixed with concern. "I helped you because I could not let them kill you. You're important to me . . . to my brother," he corrected.

Her cheeks flushed pink as she turned to face the trees. Silence settled between them as they made their way back to the others.

When they arrived at the campsite, it was to see Moreis and Lachlan pacing back and forth. The horses had been saddled and the supplies returned to their packs. Quinn brought Odin to a stop.

Gillis ran to greet them, her eyes wide as she took in their blood-splattered garments. "What did they do tae her?"

"She's well," Quinn assured the maid.

"You're not," Lachlan said, his gaze moving to the open wound at Quinn's shoulder.

The wound was not bleeding profusely and would no doubt heal in time. "I've suffered worse."

Moreis stopped in front of Odin and drew his sword. "What about her captors? Are they still in pursuit? Do we fight?"

"They are no longer a threat," Quinn assured the others.

Lachlan lifted his arms to receive Vivian, slowly lowering her to the ground. Vivian swayed when she gained her feet, then braced as Gillis thrust herself into the younger woman's arms.

"Pray tell, what happened?" the maid asked, scowling at the traces of blood on her mistress's clothing.

"It was my fault," Vivian acknowledged. "I went looking for Quinn. But instead of finding him I encountered hunters seeking me for a bounty."

"What insanity possessed ye, woman?" Moreis asked as he took Odin's reins.

Vivian resisted the urge to tell them she'd tried to wake them. The knowledge would serve no purpose other than to ease her own guilt.

Quinn jumped down. "What's done is done. Vivian is safe."

"Damn fool woman." Moreis wasn't ready to let the matter go as he fixed Vivian with a scowl. "Ye could've been killed."

"You are right," Vivian said, clasping her hands around her upper arms. She hesitated and her brow furrowed. "There is more you should know." She sighed, suddenly concentrating on the ground at her feet.

She had been about to tell them something important, Quinn was certain. "What should we know?" he prompted.

When she lifted her gaze once more her expression was grim. "My foolishness cost a man his life and injured Quinn's shoulder. You are all at risk if you stay with me. No task is worth you putting yourselves in mortal danger."

With a mix of exasperation and irritation, Quinn drew a long, harsh breath and said curtly, "We all knew this assignment would not be without challenges, but it is our duty to see it through." Quinn turned away from her. "Gillis, help your mistress change into the gown you brought her. We need to keep going if we are to reach Inishail Convent."

"Then you will take me there?" Vivian asked with hope in her voice.

"Against my better judgment, but aye," Quinn said, suddenly feeling the effects of too many sleepless nights weighing upon him. "Only to rest if you can promise me your abbess will take us in for temporary refuge?"

"Aye. I'd trust Abbess Catherine with my life, and yours," Vivian replied, offering him a sincere smile. "She and the others will watch over us so you can finally sleep, and there I will take a look at that wound."

Quinn shook his head, fighting the effect of her smile upon him. For a moment it had felt as though sunlight had touched his face. It was simply his exhaustion playing tricks on him. If he didn't sleep soon, he'd be of no use to anyone. "I'm trusting you with our lives."

Vivian's smile widened. "You won't be disappointed."

CHAPTER SEVEN

ECKONING ON THE horizon like ancient twisted hands
B were the mist-ridden peaks of the Grampian Mountains. They formed a wall of hostile, seemingly impenetrable rock that stood between the Highlands and the Lowlands. At the base of the bluish mountains, nestled in a sea of green, stood Inishail Convent.

Vivian should have been filled with joy upon seeing the gleaming buff-colored walls in the distance, yet she felt only exhaustion. The sun was beginning to set, painting the sky with a reddish-orange glow. The path they had followed skirted the banks of Loch Awe. Mist gathered in places along the lowland pasture, making it appear as if they were riding into an opaque wall. The air smelled fresh and filled with the promise that things were starting to change in their favor.

"You did not mention your convent was so fine," Quinn said from behind her on Odin's back.

"I had forgotten," Vivian replied, eyeing the perfectly proportioned structure nestled in a setting that was the epitome of tranquility. "I came here as a little girl, and that was long ago." A lifetime ago when her mother had still lived.

It was here at Inishail that her mother had died. She'd left Vivian alone in the world at the age of nine with no one to explain what her visions meant or how to contend with the havoc they would cause in her life.

Once, Vivian had tried to explain to then-Sister Catherine what she had seen in her mind's eye. Later, after the event had come to pass, Sister Catherine had taken her aside and warned her never to reveal her gift to anyone, saying most people would not understand or forgive Vivian for such predictions about the future. Vivian had had a few more visions after that, one with a terrifying end, then as abruptly as they'd started, her visions had stopped for the next four years. She'd lived happily among the nuns, contributing to the welfare of the group by learning to use local herbs to create brews and salves that healed the sisters.

It wasn't until she was thirteen that her visions resumed and turned her life upside down all over again when she saw herself at the Scottish court.

The next day the king's man arrived at the convent, claiming he'd been sent by King James himself to bring her back to his court. In spite of the newly appointed Abbess Catherine's pleas, the king's man took Vivian away.

As Quinn brought the horse to a stop at the convent's wrought-iron gate, Vivian shook off the memories of her past. "Let me down," Vivian said. "'Tis best if I talk with the gatekeeper about who we are and why we're here."

Quinn dismounted and lifted Vivian to the ground. "I'll be here if you need me," he assured her in a low voice.

The words were comforting as she rang the small bell beside the gate bearing a black cross at the top. The clang of the bell hung in the air for a long moment before a woman in a white habit, white scapular, and black veil shuffled toward them.

The woman stopped at the gate without opening it. "Blessings of our Lord to you," she greeted. "How might I be of service?"

At first Vivian did not recognize the nun until the woman raised her chin and studied them over the bridge of her nose. "Sister Mary Margaret? 'Tis I, Vivian Sinclair . . . Lady Campbell . . . as of late. My friends and I seek shelter for the night."

The nun's face crumpled as tears came to her eyes. "Lord's mercy, Vivian?"

"Aye."

The older nun had been like a second mother to Vivian while she'd stayed at the convent.

The nun's eyes widened as a joyous expression deepened the wrinkles in her face. "We feared we would never see you again." With shaking fingers, she reached for the keys chained to her belt and rustled through them until she found the wrought-iron key that opened the gate. Swinging the barrier aside, she pulled Vivian into an embrace. "We missed you, little angel."

"I missed you, too," Vivian said, the words tight in her throat. "May I introduce my friends?"

Sister Mary Margaret released Vivian but kept hold of her hand, as though unable to part with a person she'd thought she'd lost long ago. The nun's gaze shifted to Quinn and then the others behind him while Vivian made the introductions.

"Any friends of yours are welcome here. Come and bring the horses. We have a stable around back." The nun stepped aside, taking Vivian with her. Sister Mary Margaret waved the rest of the traveling party through the gates. When they were all within the convent walls, the nun dropped Vivian's hand and set about locking the gate behind them. "Vespers are just concluding. Your arrival is very timely."

Quinn's dark eyes swept their surroundings, as though searching for dangers even here among the nuns.

"No one can reach us here." Vivian released a pent-up breath and the tension inside her eased, leaving her feeling suddenly weak and wobbly.

Quinn reached for her arm, steadying her. "It is a habit, I'm afraid. I am always on guard."

Sister Mary Margaret finished locking the gate and turned to face Vivian with a frown. "Are you well, little angel?"

"I will be, after a meal and some rest," Vivian said more steadily than she felt. "The important thing is that we are here."

"And safe," Sister Mary Margaret said. At Vivian's questioning glance she added, "It has been many years since you were last here, but I know the look of despair when I see it. It is not just on your face that I see exhaustion and worry." The older woman's perceptive gaze shifted to Quinn, then Moreis, Lachlan, and finally Gillis. "It appears all of you are in need of some Inishail hospitality and a good night's sleep."

"We are indebted to you for your kindness," Quinn said. His features were still uneasy as they made their way through the courtyard surrounded by cloisters.

Sister Mary Margaret smiled at Quinn as they walked within the arched walkway toward the main area of the convent. "There is no greater gift than seeing our little angel again," she said, her keys jangling against her hip with each step as she hurried along the walkway. "Before we head to the frater for your evening meal, I must present you to Mother Abbess. She can usually be found in the chapter house after prayers. But before we go in, I request that you leave your weapons here. You'll have no need of them within the convent walls."

Quinn frowned but did as the sister asked, pulling his sword from his scabbard and setting the blade on the stone ledge beside the door. "I will keep my dagger."

"If you so choose," Sister Mary Margaret said.

The other men followed suit. Once they were done, they entered the candle-lit chamber to find the abbess sitting in front of a desk, her veil-covered head bent over a ledger.

Vivian stopped just inside the doorway as the abbess looked up. She studied each of the visitors until her gaze lit on Vivian. Her eyes widened and a smile came to her lips. She stood and came around the desk. "I am sorry for whatever troubles brought you here, yet I must say it fills me with joy to see you again."

Vivian rushed forward and threw herself into Abbess Catherine's arms. "As you guessed, I am in terrible trouble, but all that seems so far away now that I am here."

"And your companions?" the abbess asked.

Vivian pulled back and turned to the others. "This is Quinn Douglas, his men Moreis and Lachlan, and my maid, Gillis."

When Vivian introduced Gillis, the maid's lashes lowered to veil her eyes. Vivian frowned at Gillis's odd response, but as Quinn stepped forward, her attention returned to him.

"Mother Abbess, it is very gracious of you to receive us," Quinn replied with a bow of his head.

"We receive all who are troubled here," the abbess said, eyeing the dried blood at Quinn's temple and shoulder through narrowed eyes. "I believe you are in need of care for those wounds?"

"My wounds are not deep, and I believe other needs are far more important at the moment, such as food and sleep." He shrugged off the unwanted attention, but Vivian knew his injuries, especially the one at his shoulder, were far worse than he let on. It was not a premonition that told her so, yet she had the same unsettling sensation in the core of her being she usually had before a vision. If left untreated, his wound would become putrid.

"I will see to his injuries as soon as we are shown to the guest house," Vivian said.

"I'm well enough," Quinn grumbled.

An amused smile lit Abbess Catherine's face as her gaze shifted between Vivian and Quinn. "Sister Mary Margaret will see you to supper, then to the guest house. After that—" her tone sobered "—Vivian will tend your wounds."

Quinn opened his mouth to protest.

The abbess stopped him with a raised hand. "I realize the Douglas family prides itself on taking care of its own, but in this instance, I must demand you surrender yourself to Vivian's care. She was an excellent healer when she left us years ago. I can only imagine her skills have grown in that time."

Quinn bowed, then stepped back toward the door. "As you wish, Mother Abbess."

"Sister Mary Margaret, please escort our guests to the evening meal," the abbess said.

While the others followed the nun back outside, Abbess Catherine detained Vivian with a touch on her sleeve. "You can join them in a moment. You and I have a few things to discuss."

Vivian watched Quinn's retreating back. She heard the

crunch of his boots on the cobblestones as he moved quickly across the courtyard. She felt suddenly hollow, as if he had taken some part of her with him. What an idiotic thought, she told herself. Nothing had been taken from her. Quinn had simply been a big part of her every moment for the past two days. It was only natural she would feel a little drained and flat at his departure. Vivian shook her head, casting off her bemusement. "I thought you wanted me to heal him."

"The dried blood on his shirt suggests he was injured a while ago. I suspect he can wait a little longer while you and I converse. If I'm to shelter you and your friends, I need to know what trouble may find its way here." The abbess waved Vivian toward an empty chair beside the desk.

Vivian sat tentatively on the edge of the chair. "How much do you know about my life after the convent?" News traveled from the Scottish court to all parts of the country eventually, even to an isolated convent like Inishail.

"I never would have allowed you to leave here if I hadn't had someone close to keep an eye on your safety."

Vivian startled. "What do you mean? There was no one."

A satisfied smile came to the abbess's face. "Your governess at court and your maid at Kilkerran Castle were both employed by us to keep watch over you."

"Mistress Pearson and Gillis?" Vivian was too overwhelmed to say more.

The abbess's brow creased. "When you were forced to marry Dugald Campbell, it came as a bit of a surprise. Before we could do anything to intercede, the deed had been done. You seemed content enough, so we let things be. Yet here you are traveling without your husband."

"Dugald died two days ago."

The crease deepened and the abbess's eyes filled with sympathy. "Gillis never informed us. I'm so sorry, Vivian. Do you mourn his loss?"

"Though he was kindly, honestly, nay, because he suffered toward the end."

"And Quinn Douglas?" the abbess asked as the expression on her face shifted to curiosity. "Did you become acquainted at Kilkerran?"

"We met the day Dugald died."

The abbess frowned. "How is that possible? He seems very concerned for your welfare."

"What you see is only his overactive sense of duty." Vivian dropped her gaze to her feet, hiding the heat she could feel rising in her cheeks.

"I'm confused," the abbess admitted. "If you did not know him from Kilkerran, then what duty does he have toward you?"

Vivian looked up. The last thing she wanted was to get hemmed in a corner by others' expectations of her. She and Quinn were together at the convent because he'd escorted her there. Beyond taking her to his brother, there was nothing more. "Quinn and I do not have a future together, if that is what you're wondering. The king is once again forcing me into marriage, to Quinn's brother."

The abbess frowned. "Then why did his brother not come for you?"

"Quinn said it was because his brother was in service to the king and could not abandon his task." Vivian lifted her chin. "I suspect the man finds having a wife as inconvenient as I do a husband."

Abbess Catherine's brow rose. "A true marriage would be different than what you and Dugald had."

Vivian raised her chin. "I do not care to repeat my mother and father's past."

At her comment the abbess tilted her mouth to one side. "You're a very different person than either your mother or father. Do not base your life choices on what they did or did not have."

Vivian frowned. "I cannot see a different way forward where marriage is concerned."

"You've had a vision of your future life?" the abbess asked with a questioning look.

"Nay," Vivian acknowledged.

"You promised me once you would keep an open mind about marriage and a possible family of your own."

"I have not seen or experienced anything that would sway my opinion."

"Then you've not yet met the person who will convince you otherwise," the abbess replied, keeping her gaze fixed on Vivian. "That's neither here nor there. In your current situation, it is obvious Quinn cares for you even if you are only just acquainted."

"Quinn rescued me . . . on more than one occasion. I suspect it is the peril we have survived together that makes us seem more familiar than we are."

"The question still remains, why are you in trouble in the first place?" As it had in the past, Abbess Catherine's gaze became eagle-eyed sharp. "Your visions are the cause, are they not?"

"Aye. My visions are always the cause of my trouble and my biggest fears." At the memory of her one-time friend, a chill settled inside Vivian, as cold as winter, as sharp as a knife.

"Sister Emmelia's death was not your fault."

Vivian forced herself to pull in a breath as the past rumbled through her mind. Shortly after arriving at the convent, she'd had a vision of herself and her new friend Emmelia gathering herbs outside the convent walls when a rainstorm had drenched them both, leading to Emmelia catching a cold that weakened her lungs for the rest of her life. Feeling empowered by the knowledge of what was to happen, Vivian had waited until later that afternoon when the rain had passed and the sun peeked out from behind the clouds.

And just when Vivian had thought everything was perfect, that her visions might somehow be a gift for altering the future, Emmelia had slipped down a hillside and plunged into the swollen river below. Caught in the rapids, she'd drowned before Vivian could reach her friend. The cold settled deeper, pinching Vivian's lungs. "If I hadn't tried to change what I'd seen—"

"It was God's will for Emmelia to leave this earth that day. As I've reminded you before, your vision was not the cause."

After that day, Vivian had never tried to change the entirety of a vision again. She'd prayed for days that her visions would leave her. And as if in answer to those prayers, they had for a while.

"Since leaving us, who have you told about your abilities?" Abbess Catherine asked.

"I told the king shortly after arriving at his court when I had a vision of his death at the hands of an assassin."

Abbess Catherine's brow furrowed. "You stopped the attempt?"

"In a manner of speaking. After telling the king about Emmelia, I convinced him to go through with his public address, yet dressed him in armor. The arrow that was meant for him no longer found its mark and the king was safe." Vivian tilted her head in thought. "I believe that incident is why he always saw my abilities as a gift instead of something evil. They had benefitted him."

"And the king told no one else?"

Vivian frowned. "The king told Dugald, but I trust he kept that information to himself." It was a secret that had to be hidden. Vivian brought her fingers up to her temples, smoothing the skin as she might during one of her visions. She'd almost revealed her gift to Quinn and the others today before she'd caught herself.

"Then I suspect you're in trouble because of your skills as a healer that some might mistake as witchcraft."

Vivian nodded. "Dugald's son Rupert is the reason for that. He's the crown's Witch Hunter and his gaze is focused on me. He must have made the villagers of Kilkerran doubt me and my healing abilities. One of them called me a witch. Three of them followed me as far as Tarbert in order to claim the bounty on my head."

The abbess's face paled. "That's when Quinn was injured. Protecting you from them?"

Vivian nodded.

Abbess Catherine's expression turned grim. "Others will come looking for you, won't they?"

"I fear so," Vivian said.

The older woman stood. "Now it is time for you to rejoin the others. We'll talk more on the morrow. I must think and pray about what to do. And you need food and sleep."

Vivian surged to her feet, suddenly eager to be back among the others. "Aye." She caught the abbess's curious gaze and continued quickly, "For the others' sake, of course."

"Of course," the abbess echoed softly.

Suddenly breathless at the thought of returning to Quinn's side, Vivian said, "Until the morrow."

She made her way toward the door and hurried along the

familiar path across the cobblestones until she found the others in the dining room. The room was unchanged since she'd seen it last. Four long wooden tables with several benches tucked beneath stretched from end-to-end in the room. Each table held two candelabras and several bowls of wrinkly apples. At the table closest to the door sat Moreis, Lachlan, and Gillis. They were the only people in the frater with Sister Mary Margaret. Judging by the aroma, they had just finished a simple meal of rabbit stew and crusty bread.

"I'm glad Mother Abbess didn't keep you too long." The nun turned to Vivian with a welcoming smile.

The three travelers stood and stacked their wooden bowls on a tray held by Sister Mary Margaret. "Your friend Quinn has already retired. I don't think he was feeling well. He seemed dreadfully tired." She shrugged. "I was just getting ready to take the others to the guest house. Would you like us to wait for you while you have something to eat?" Sister Mary Margaret asked.

Vivian shook her head as thoughts of Quinn filled her mind. "I'm not hungry."

Sister Mary Margaret set the tray on the long wooden table before her and took an apple from the bowl closest to her. "At least take this for later," the nun said with concern.

Vivian accepted the offering and swallowed to ease the sudden tightness in her throat. It had been a long while since anyone had cared about her welfare. "Thank you."

She slipped the apple into the waist pouch where she

kept her important herbs hidden beneath the folds of her skirt. Then she fell into step beside the others as they made their way to their sleeping quarters. The guest house was on the opposite side of the convent from the dormitory where the nuns slept in small cells on mattresses of straw, in keeping with their vows of chastity, poverty, and obedience. Guests, however, were not required to follow such an austere observance. The beds in the guest house, while still simple feather beds, were luxurious by comparison.

When Sister Mary Margaret swung the wooden door open, Vivian was reminded that in addition to a great room at the center, the guest house had several bedrooms within. "Moreis and Lachlan, we've prepared the room on the right for the two of you. Gillis and Vivian, you'll take the room on the left."

"Where's Quinn?" Vivian asked, trying not to sound too eager to see the man. "If I'm to heal his wounds, I'll need to know where he is."

Sister Mary Margaret nodded. "I put him in the room over there." She pointed to the closed door farther down the hallway. "If you need any supplies—"

"I remember where to find most things, but if you could send some hot water and clean linen I would be most grateful," Vivian interrupted, eager to get on with her duties. "The man's lifeblood could be pouring out onto the floor as we speak."

Moreis and Lachlan looked puzzled while Gillis gasped.

"I didna know his wound was that serious."

Vivian had exaggerated for her own purpose, but she had their attention now and she intended to use it to her advantage. "Quinn needs all of our help to make him well."

"Oh, heavens." Sister Mary Margaret's eyes widened. "We don't want him falling ill or dying. I'll have water to you in no time."

When the nun left, Moreis came to Vivian's side. "Quinn's a hardy lad. Don't ye be worryin' yerself over him."

Undeterred, Vivian straightened and looked the older man in the eyes despite the fact that the top of her head barely reached his shoulder. "I'm the one who rode with him here. I could feel the heat steadily increasing in his body as the day advanced. His wounded shoulder is primed to turn putrid. If I don't attend him soon, he might just die."

Moreis's face turned pale as he shook his shaggy head. "What can I do tae help?"

"Get the bags from the horses. If you have a new shirt for Quinn, that would be helpful. His current garment is ruined."

Moreis didn't hesitate. In the next instant he began snapping orders not just to Lachlan about bringing in the supplies from the stable, but he sent Gillis running after Sister Mary Margaret to see if she could hasten the process of boiling water. When the door slammed closed behind them, Vivian hurried to Quinn's room.

No harm would come to him, not on her watch.

CHAPTER EIGHT

RUPERT CAMPBELL FUMED at the news of Vivian's escape. All the effort he'd put into having that witch captured after she'd left the castle had failed. His hands tightened on the reins of his horse as he waited for yet another group of men he'd employed to find her. Where his own guards and the village peasants had failed, these mercenary hunters would succeed.

Vivian had last been seen outside Tarbert. The only two directions for her to go were either to the north or northeast. The terrain heading north into the Grampian Mountains, with deep glens and sheer cliffs, would be brutal at any time of the year. It would be especially so in the spring due to rain, leaving the ground boggy and unpredictable.

He and his men would head northeast. If she was anywhere in the area, they would find and destroy her.

Rupert looked off into the distance, toward the setting sun. He hadn't always been such a brutal man. Once he'd been a devoted son of the Campbell clan. Until his own mother had consulted a witch, asking for bewitched images to kill her son and husband. She'd almost succeeded in killing Rupert. The scars on his chest were proof of that. Yet his father would never believe that the woman he'd married was capable of such a thing.

Rupert had no trouble believing, especially after he consulted the same witch, Norma Croft, and had acquired toad's venom that he'd slipped into his mother's ale one night, causing her death. Ten years later, when Rupert had come of age and had worked his way into the role of sheriff of Haddingtonshire, he went back to Kilkerran for Norma Croft. She'd been the first woman he'd convicted and hanged as a witch. There had been fourteen other witches he'd exposed and punished since.

Rupert clenched his jaw as everything in him tightened with determination. The search for evil continued even now with Vivian. No woman should have the power to alter a man's fate, especially no woman who could foretell the future.

He knew her secret. His father had told him about Vivian's visions the night before he'd died. While Vivian had been talking with her maid, his father had tried to convince him that Vivian's abilities were good and useful. A glimpse into the future could offer a man many benefits. Unless those glimpses were created from pure evil, which they were.

The woman was a witch. Vivian's abilities might have saved her from burning at the stake before now. All that would change once he and his men found her.

And when he did, he would show her no mercy, just as

his mother had never shown mercy to him.

QUINN OPENED HIS eyes to see Vivian frowning down at him with determination. The look was strangely more comforting than tenderness would have been.

"I was hoping not to wake you," she said.

The candelabra she'd brought with her into the chamber cast a warm, golden glow on her red hair, making her look more like a spirit than a flesh and blood woman. Yet when she gently stroked his forehead with a cool cloth, she seemed very real, indeed, even as her image wavered before him.

"Your fever is growing, meaning your wound has turned putrid."

A dull ache had settled in his shoulder. And even though he was feverishly warm, he shivered.

"I need to reopen your wound and drain it. It will hurt, but there are ways of making the pain less intense."

"Whiskey?" he asked, hopefully.

She shook her head. "The nuns have no spirits here. Only mead."

"Mead will do."

She set her cloth aside and poured him a mug of the golden liquid.

He accepted the mug and drank it. When he was done, she set the mug aside and took both of his hands in her own.

"I need you to try to think of something beautiful."

"I cannot at present think of anything," Quinn said dryly despite the fact that the most beautiful thing he'd seen in a long time stood before him, holding his hands. Quinn was drawn by the sheer intensity of her manner. When she was in her natural element and not scared out of her wits, she was a sight to behold. Her blue eyes were brilliant, sparkling with vitality in her slender face. The high color of her cheeks glowed rose against cream skin.

"You must," Vivian said fiercely. "What's the most beautiful thing you've ever seen?"

"The Scottish sea."

She drew her hands from his and gently peeled his blood-crusted shirt away from the wound. "Then think of the sea. Tell me about it. What do you remember?"

Searing pain shot through his shoulder, followed by pressure. "A recent . . . storm. It sent waves . . . dashing against the ship with curling fingers of foam." He drew a sharp breath, then released it, feeling more in control. "The sound of the fury . . . was as beautiful . . . as the mighty waves crashing against the hull."

"What else?"

Her voice was calm, melodic. He focused on the sound, allowing it to calm him as Vivian pressed a warm cloth against his flesh, washing away the dried blood. "When the water is calm it turns a deep, shimmering green that sparkles in the—" White-hot pain stabbed his shoulder again as a cool liquid replaced the warmth. Then there was pressure—lots of pressure.

"Remember the sea." Her blue eyes held the pain at bay.

He moistened his lips with his tongue. "On a calm day, as the ship nears the shore, it's like floating on a smooth emerald. It's breathtaking." But not nearly as breathtaking as her skin, glowing in the candlelight.

Pain exploded in his shoulder as a blade cut through his flesh. Quinn arched up, the room suddenly whirling around him. He felt the warm flow of his own blood trickle down his shoulder.

"That's the worst of it," Vivian whispered as she cupped the side of his face with her hand. With a soft smile, she removed her hand to once again wipe at his shoulder with a warm cloth. "I need to let the wound bleed freely for a few moments to make certain it will not become putrid again."

Quinn sank back against the bed, mourning the loss of her touch. Strange. He'd never accepted solace from a woman before. "You seem to know what you're doing," he said through another stab of pain. "As far as I could tell," he forced a laugh as he continued, "there was no witchcraft involved."

Instead of participating in his humor, Vivian's face flushed in distress.

Quinn instantly regretted his words.

"There is no magic in what I do." Her features shuttered as she looked away, continuing to clean the blood from his wound. "By tomorrow your wound will be healed over. It will take a few days more for you to fully recover and for your strength to return."

Quinn hadn't meant his words as any kind of slight, but she'd taken them as such. He would have to be more careful in the future. "I thought I knew all about healers," he said humbly. "I was wrong. You are unusual, but in the very best of ways. I thank you for your care."

Surprise flared in the depths of her eyes as she continued to tend his wound. "Think back on the waves as they crash against the hull of your ship." Her voice was sweet, luring him into a state of relaxation. "It's time to stanch the bleeding with stitches. This could hurt," she said as she poked the needle into his skin and sewed the two edges of his flesh together with silken thread.

He tensed then relaxed as he focused his mind not on the sea, but on the way her long red hair cascaded across her slim shoulders to fall against her back.

When she had finished, she cleaned his wound with a fresh cloth. "I've treated many people for a variety of ailments. Not many men would have borne the pain you did without crying out."

A faint smile came to his lips. "I had no need to cry out. As you bid me, I was thinking of something . . . beautiful."

AFTER HOURS OF sitting at Quinn's bedside, Vivian straightened in the chair, arching her spine to rid it of its stiffness. The movement did little to ease her discomfort. She should really get up and walk about the chamber, but she feared waking the man lying on the bed. He'd been asleep for hours, finally giving in to his exhaustion. Even so, his sleep had been restless, which was why she'd stayed with him instead of returning to her own bed. It wouldn't do for her to tend him only to have him succumb to a fever once more.

Her gaze returned to Quinn. He no longer looked like the villainous figure she'd imagined when they'd first met. The hard angles of his face seemed softer. Before succumbing to sleep his dark eyes had no longer been hard and determined but filled with mysteries she longed to solve. He wouldn't readily give up his secrets, yet given time, she was sure she'd find a way to untangle the knot that was Quinn Douglas.

His eyes flicked open, totally alert. "What are you thinking?"

Vivian was startled to see the intensity of his gaze after so many hours of watching him sleep. She turned away from him, hiding the high color she could feel warming her cheeks. "I was hoping you were healing." When her surprise and embarrassment were back under control, she turned to him. "How do you feel?"

"Better." He frowned at the sight of her. "Have you been beside me all night? Go to bed."

"Do you think I'd go to such lengths to save you then let you die from lack of care?" She returned to the bedside and put the backs of her fingers to his brow above the bandages she had placed there, checking for evidence of a returned fever.

His gaze searched her face. "Will I live?"

"Aye." She pulled her hand away but not before he gently captured her wrist.

"Since you refuse to sleep, can we talk for a while?"

Vivian nodded.

He released his grip on her and shifted into a sitting position, wincing with pain as he stretched the wound in his shoulder. "You do not seem happy about the king's arrangement with my brother."

She returned to her chair. "I am not."

When he settled back against the pillows, his pinched features eased. "Why? I can attest to the fact that Reid will treat you well. He's been a warrior his whole life, but he is not a brutal man. He will protect you from men like Rupert Campbell."

"I do not seek a protector. If I marry again, I wish it to be on my own terms." Vivian lifted her chin, expecting him to scoff at her bold statement, especially when they both knew she had no choice in the matter.

He did not laugh. Instead he looked at her with sincerity. "What terms would those be?"

With nothing to lose she forged ahead. "I want to continue to improve my skills as a healer. I want to treat people in the outlying villages who have no access to a healer of any kind. I want to teach others how to help themselves and their people." At the thought of such freedoms, her throat tightened.

"Go on," Quinn encouraged.

She swallowed roughly. "I know what I want is unusual for a woman, but I truly believe I can help others."

He frowned. "Do you not fear what could happen to you for wanting such things? Rupert, and men like him, will always be a threat. The king has given Rupert absolute authority in witch hunting, and the hunter is wielding his power not with care, but with ruthlessness toward those who are caught in his snare."

"I have fears like everyone else, but I do not fear being different as much as I fear not using my gifts for good. We all have special gifts, every one of us. Using them for the betterment of mankind is what we should all strive for."

An odd light came to Quinn's eyes. "You are not like other women."

She felt an odd pang. His words sounded more like a compliment than a reproach. "Nay, I suppose I am not."

He set his jaw as he studied her. "I cannot promise you anything, but I will address your terms with my brother when we reach Redhouse Castle."

"That is more than I could have hoped for," she said with a genuine smile. He did not have to plead her case before his brother, but she appreciated that he would try. They both knew it would be difficult to go against the king's wishes. "Close your eyes and get some rest. Your healer demands it of you."

He wearily closed his eyes. "Stay as you like. Who am I to refuse your ministrations?"

"I'm glad you've come to your senses."

"I've done no such thing. My fever must have returned."

Filled with sudden anxiety, Vivian sprang from her chair to his side. She brought her hand to his brow only to sigh in relief. "No fever."

"Then why else have I become an irrational fool?"

Not knowing how to respond, Vivian stared down at Quinn. His eyes remained closed but he responded with a smile. Not just any smile. An arresting smile, one that did strange things to her insides.

Perhaps they were both becoming irrational fools because in that instant she wanted nothing more than to bend down and kiss him. "Sleep. It will cure all that ails you," she said as she returned to the safety of her chair.

"I doubt that, but again, as a healer you know what's best," he said mockingly.

At his words, a shiver slid through her, seeping into her bones, her soul. She had no idea what was best for her, for him, for anyone who remained in her company for too long. Rupert had proven over the last two days that his enmity wouldn't die easily.

CHAPTER NINE

THE NEXT MORNING Vivian dressed Quinn's wound with a poultice of honey then tied a fresh bandage atop the injury. "Your shoulder is healing very well. You should be able to travel soon. Perhaps by the end of the week."

"We leave on the morrow," he said without expression.

"That's too soon. You're not well enough to—"

"Believe me when I tell you I have suffered worse. It's time to move on."

"Is there anything I can say to convince you otherwise?" Vivian asked.

Quinn shook his head. "Every moment we delay only puts those who harbor us in greater danger. I need to get you to Redhouse Castle where the defenses are strong and the men primed for battle."

Vivian straightened. She knew he was right. She would never willingly do anything to put the nuns in danger. "What if I'm not ready to leave?" she objected, trying to think of a way to buy him more time to heal from his injury. Even a few hours more would help his recovery.

Quinn met her gaze. "You have what remains of the day.

Prepare yourself for that eventuality."

She nodded and started to turn away.

"It is my duty to keep you safe." He caught her hand. His grip was not firm but his touch made her pulse leap.

"Why do you care so much about my welfare? You hardly know me."

"For Reid's sake," Quinn said. "He has yet to meet you, but I am certain the two of you will suit each other well."

He spoke of his brother. Vivian stepped back, forcing him to release her. "I am more than I appear to be."

"Are we not all more than we appear?" he replied without mockery. "The king is very fond of you, Vivian. He has gone to great lengths to make certain this new marital arrangement will be an advantageous one for you."

"I am not his puppet." Vivian found her fists were clenched and forced them to relax. "Or yours."

Quinn pushed the covers back and stood before moving toward her. "Do you trust me to do what's best for you?"

She inhaled sharply. "The king trusts you. Your brother trusts you. I suppose I must."

"No, Vivian. You. Do you trust me?" He tipped her face to his with his finger so that she looked into his eyes. His thumb caressed her cheek.

A hot flush infused the skin beneath his touch. Quickly, she lowered her lashes to veil the emotions she was certain reflected in her eyes. "I trust you."

"Then know what I do, I do for your welfare," he said.

She stepped back as an odd pang moved through her. He was saying goodbye to the intimacy they'd shared since their arrival at the convent. She forced herself to look at him, then wished she hadn't. His words said one thing. The look he gave her said something else entirely.

A tingling spread from the top of her head to the soles of her feet and to every nerve and muscle in between. Her throat constricted. "I must go," she said, bolting from the room. Her face was flushed and her body trembling as she raced through the cloister, past the nuns' dormitory, to a place she remembered well: the infirmary.

At the doorway, she drew a tight breath, trying to regain some semblance of control. When her heartbeat returned to normal, she entered the empty chamber, grateful that her attention was immediately drawn to the large painting on the far wall. She'd spent many hours alone in this chamber with the painted Madonna.

"I've missed you," Vivian said to the image of the woman who sat delicately upon a golden throne with Jesus on her lap. The woman in the image was surrounded by eight angels. Beneath her feet were the four gospel writers Matthew, Mark, Luke, and John. A profusion of gold dominated all else.

The painting would have been better suited to the chapel. Yet the convent's most priceless religious icon resided here in the infirmary where only the sick or the dying could bask in its splendor. That suited Vivian just fine as she donned an apron and looked about the empty room.

All eight of the beds were perfectly made. The stone floor was spotless. All the herbs she'd used in the past were neatly labeled and placed on shelves at the left side of the chamber. Moving closer to the worktable beside the shelves, Vivian saw the only sign that someone had been in this chamber recently. A pestle lay in the center of the worktable next to its matching mortar. Stems of dried alfalfa were discarded nearby.

Vivian brought the mortar to her nose. She smelled alfalfa, comfrey, blackberry, and nettles. Someone had made a tisane to combat the pain that sometimes accompanied a woman's monthly flux. "Who still remains at the convent who can do such things?" she asked the image on the wall.

"Your old teacher. That's who."

Vivian set the mortar down and turned with a smile to see Sister Agnes coming through the doorway toward her. It had been six years since she'd seen the older woman. She hadn't changed much. She was still plump, with rosy cheeks, and deep wrinkles at the sides of her eyes and at the corners of her mouth. That smile was still ever present as was a hint of laughter in her gray eyes.

"You're a blessed sight to behold," Vivian said, pushing an errant tendril of her hair from her face.

Sister Agnes opened her arms as she approached. "Your hair is as wild as ever."

"It has always had a mind of its own." Vivian's tension

eased. She embraced the older woman. "How I've missed you, Sister Agnes."

"Likewise, my dear." The white-haired nun stepped back but held on to Vivian's arms, searching her from head to toe. "You're all grown up, and very beautiful."

Vivian blushed at the compliment. "It's been many years. So much has changed."

Sister Agnes's eyes darkened. "I learned this morning of your misfortune, and also your good fortune to be in the care of that handsome Quinn Douglas, if Sister Mary Margaret is to be believed. I almost came to attend you both this morning but I figured you had the young man's care well in hand." The nun's gaze narrowed. "So now you must tell me, is it true? Is he handsome?"

Vivian's mouth opened then closed before she finally replied, "Aye, perhaps a little."

"A little? That's not what Mary Margaret said."

A peculiar pang tightened Vivian's chest. "All right. He's handsome. And kind. Is that what you wanted to hear?"

Sister Agnes's smile broadened. "Aye. He'll make you a fine husband."

"Quinn is not my intended. His brother is."

The nun's brow furrowed. "That cannot be. Sister Mary Margaret said—"

"Can we please speak of something else?" Vivian stepped back, out of the nun's arms and looked about the chamber for a means of distraction. "Are there new potions you could teach me? New herbs that you've discovered the medicinal properties of? Is anyone presently sick and in need of care?" Vivian winced at the breathless tone of her voice. She had to regain her equilibrium. Simply speaking of Quinn brought back the memory of his touch upon her cheek and the look in his eyes.

Sister Agnes gazed at her, puzzled. "I could teach you a few new tisanes." She walked to the shelves and took down a dark brown vial. After picking up a clean cloth, she brought the vial to Vivian. "This is something I concocted for you . . . for your past headaches, but I have also used it to treat Sister Collette for her hysteria."

Sister Agnes knew nothing of Vivian's visions. Instead, whenever she'd had one in the nun's presence, Vivian had explained her odd behavior and the following pain as severe headaches. "What is it?" Vivian asked, removing the stopper and sniffing the contents.

"What do you smell?"

"It smells both sour and sweet . . . like vinegar and rose water."

The nun smiled. "Aye, but also with a touch of treacle and a few drops of laudanum."

Vivian replaced the stopper. "How do you administer the treatment?"

"Through the skin of the forehead."

Vivian was grateful such a strong tonic was not ingested. She handed the vial back to the nun. Such a mixture would only make Vivian's visions worse. "Does it help Sister Collette?"

"Very much. She hasn't had an episode for two years." Replacing the vial, the older woman withdrew another clear jar of dried powder. "This might interest you."

Vivian accepted the jar and removed the lid, releasing the scent of the fragrant herbs. "I smell marjoram and thyme, and something else."

"Wormwood and marigold petals."

Vivian frowned. "I'm not familiar with the healing properties of such a combination. What does it do?"

"'Tis a love potion." A dimple appeared in Sister Agnes's cheek. "Take it. Use it on your Quinn. Then he'll be sure to want you for himself."

Vivian replaced the lid and returned the jar to the shelf herself. "I have no need for such a thing." She turned to face Sister Agnes. "Why do you have such a potion in a place such as this?"

The older woman's face softened. "Four or five times a year a young maid has come to us, seeking refuge after a broken heart." She nodded toward the shelf. "My potion has helped many of those young girls find their heart's desire. It could help you, too."

"What I desire has nothing to do with any man."

Sister Agnes regarded her skeptically. "If that is what you wish to believe, then so be it." Straightening, she asked, "Would you like to see the greenhouse garden I added after you left? I am growing rare herbs. The dwarf milkwort increases milk flow in female sheep, cows, and humans. My most precious lady slipper orchid when dried and taken as a tisane helps to strengthen the stomach, heat the blood, cure a sore throat, and gladden the heart. Only the milkwort is in bloom at present. We can harvest that for you to add to your collection of herbs. And, you are welcome to take some of my dried orchid with you when you leave us."

"I would like that," Vivian replied as she followed Sister Agnes outdoors. The air was warm as they walked along a flagstone path toward the back of the convent. The slight breeze sent wisps of her hair to tease her cheeks, reminding her of the featherlight caress Quinn had placed there a short time ago. She shook off the memory as an odd sound suddenly punctuated the air.

Sister Agnes's ever-present smile vanished. "I've not heard that sound in many years."

"Swords," Vivian said, giving a name to the noise.

The two women hurried toward the sound. They round-ed a corner and came to a grassy field in front of the stable. Vivian's steps slowed. She stopped at the sight before her. Quinn and Lachlan were engaged in a rigorous session of swordplay.

Lachlan charged Quinn. A clash of metal reverberated through the air as Quinn met the thrust with one of his own, then twisted upward and sideways, putting his injured shoulder to the test. The move sent Lachlan off-balance, then down to the ground.

"Well done," Sister Agnes called out, her smile once more in place.

Quinn's head snapped up. He responded with a smile. Not just any smile. An arresting smile. A disarming smile. One that made Vivian's legs weak and sent her heartbeat into an erratic flutter.

Beside her Sister Agnes chuckled. "Heaven's mercy. Sister Mary Margaret was right. He is handsome."

Quinn offered Lachlan a hand up, then strode to Vivian and Sister Agnes, his smile shifting to something more intimate, as though he too had remembered what they'd shared. Vivian tried to look away but failed. She swallowed roughly as he drew near. "You can use your shoulder."

"I can." The words were simple, but the look in his eyes spoke of something more complex. "I could not leave until I knew I could defend you if necessary. Lachlan has proven that I can."

She found any desire to protest their leaving had abandoned her. All that mattered now was that Quinn was healing, and that once they left the nuns would be safe from Rupert and his vengeance. "We should leave you to your practice."

Quinn nodded and took a step back. "Sister Mary Margaret has informed me that she is preparing a banquet in our honor this evening in order to send us off in style."

"Then I shall see you at banquet," Vivian said then

forced herself to turn away, heading back toward the greenhouse as she and Sister Agnes had originally intended.

"I might not be very worldly when it comes to men, but if a man who was not my intended looked at me that way, I would move heaven and earth to see that I spent the rest of my life with him."

She had sworn off the shackles of marriage and motherhood, yet in that moment thinking about such things did not bring the resistance it had in the past. Vivian frowned. "It doesn't matter. The king has other plans for me."

"Then the king needs to revisit his plans because whether you admit it or not, there is a connection between you and Quinn."

"Enough, Sister Agnes," Vivian pleaded, bringing her fingers up to massage her suddenly aching temple. The cause of her pain was not a vision, but the incessant challenge put to her by her one-time mentor. "Instead of clipping herbs, I suddenly find myself in need of some quiet."

Sister Agnes nodded. "You'll find all the quiet you need in the chapel, my dear. Perhaps some reflection might help you see things more clearly."

"The chapel is an excellent idea." A few hours on her knees in the chapel with the other nuns would help her regain her equilibrium and her perspective. Such torment had always worked for her in the past when Abbess Catherine had challenged her to "better" herself.

She and Quinn had no future together because he was

both honorable and loyal, and he would never betray his brother. It was she who had stated she did not want to be tied to a man, through marriage or desire. It was time she remembered that, even if Quinn's very presence sent her heartbeat fluttering.

CHAPTER TEN

AFTER SEVERAL HOURS of failing to find solitude in the chapel, Vivian made her way on aching knees outside once more. The gardens of Inishail Convent were not large by any means, but what there were could definitely be considered magnificent. The trees were old, large and full-canopied, and cast a flickering display of sunlight and shadow onto the ornamental shrubberies below. A path meandered through the expanse, adorned by garden beds with flowers in the first blush of blooms, including Vivian's favorite: bluebells.

She bent down beside a patch of the spring flowers. She plucked a stalk and brought the bell-shaped petals to her nose, indulging in the fresh scent.

"Their fragrance is stronger and much sweeter in the early morning hours."

Vivian looked up to see Abbess Catherine standing not far from her. How had the nun approached so quietly? Or it was more likely that Vivian had been so lost in her own thoughts she'd failed to hear the woman approach. "What are you doing out here?"

"Looking for you." The older nun came closer. "You always did come to the garden when you had something on your mind."

Vivian stood. "For years I tried going to the chapel and spending hours on my knees, but to no avail. Yet a leisurely walk in the garden always brought me the clarity I sought."

"Do not apologize for such. Communing with God does not only happen in front of a cross." Abbess Catherine reached out to gently touch Vivian's cheek. "What troubles you, my dear?"

Vivian frowned. "I haven't allowed my thoughts to solidify into words."

The nun nodded. "Then let us walk and see what comes from our efforts."

The two women fell into step together, moving slowly down the path in silence. Eventually, Vivian admitted, "I don't know what I'm supposed to do anymore. I don't know how I'm supposed to feel."

"About?" the abbess prodded.

Vivian drew a deep breath as her emotions veered from fear to anguish and back again. "About marrying again, especially to a man I've never met. Putting those I travel with in danger. Being called a witch instead of a healer. Having feelings for a man I hardly know. Worrying that Rupert Campbell might capture me. Dying . . . before I've had a chance to live." Her words tapered off into silence.

After a long pause Abbess Catherine stopped and turned

toward Vivian. "The burden of any difficulty is your desire to avoid it. Have you considered how things might change if you choose instead to accept that difficulty, endure it, or to thrive on it instead?"

Vivian's frown increased. "I should accept death?"

"Death is inevitable for all of us. But if you stop worrying about whatever end awaits you, you open yourself for more of what life has to offer in the moment."

"Opening myself up could come at great cost."

The nun shrugged. "Fulfilling your potential will come with some pain, discomfort, and frustration, but through those difficulties you will grow, progress, and achieve great things."

Warmth filled Abbess Catherine's eyes. "Life is difficult and yet the rewards are great. Love is one such reward."

"Love?" Vivian objected.

Any further discussion was silenced by the abbess's raised hand. "I am not only speaking of romantic love. Healing is an act of love for everyone who receives your gift. Friendship is a form of love. Protection, the kind your Quinn offers you, is an expression of love."

Vivian felt a hot flush rush to her cheeks. "He is not *my* Quinn."

"Have faith, my dear. Quinn was brought into your life for a reason. There is a purpose to all things."

"Merciful heavens, why must you always speak in riddles?"

Abbess Catherine laughed as she reached out and touched Vivian's hand. "This hasn't been an easy time for you. First your marriage to a much older man and then your journey to meet yet another possible suitor."

"Reid Douglas is more than a suitor."

"Until you say your marriage vows, nothing is certain."

"That's almost blasphemy."

Abbess Catherine's gaze intensified. "Tell me, what is it about him that intrigues you?"

The nun spoke of Quinn, not Reid. Vivian was silent a moment before she replied, "When I'm with Quinn it's as if I'm swathed in both moonlight and sunlight at once. He makes me angry and happy at the same time."

"Interesting. Is time spent with him worthwhile?"

After a long hesitation, Vivian nodded. "Aye."

A brilliant smile lit Abbess Catherine's face. "Then unburden yourself of your fears and let whatever is supposed to happen come into being."

"My visions say otherwise." Vivian shook her head sadly. "I saw a tragic end for myself if I let destiny take its course."

Abbess Catherine set her jaw. "I cannot believe in such an outcome. The smallest of moments can change what you have seen. There is no such thing as a predestined outcome for any life, yours included. A merciful God allows you to choose from a variety of paths he has laid out before you, each with a different outcome."

"I did not actually see myself die in my vision, only the

pain I would endure."

"Not everything is as it seems, even in your visions."

Vivian was suddenly breathless. "Could you be right about this? About everything?"

"I'm not always right," the nun amended with a satisfied smile. "*Almost* always, however."

AT THE BANQUET later that night, Vivian sat at one of the long tables with an empty seat at her side, an unnecessary reminder that Quinn had chosen to remain in his chamber alone. She'd been eager to see him after her talk this afternoon with Abbess Catherine.

Perhaps his absence was for the better. Abbess Catherine might believe that any future Vivian had seen could be altered without a devastating outcome resulting from that shift. Vivian still wasn't convinced. The memory of what had happened to Sister Emmelia had dampened her spirit since this afternoon in the garden. Could she trust that things would be different this time, or that she and Quinn would ever be more than related by marriage?

Quinn had belonged to her for a few days, and in those private moments something had sparked between them. But it was too late for anything more to develop. The remainder of their journey would now be in the company of Gillis, Moreis, and Lachlan. Casual moments between Quinn and herself were now at an end.

Moreis sat across the table from Vivian, next to Gillis. The two of them were engaged in conversation that had Moreis whispering into the maid's ear, bringing a tinge of color to the older woman's cheeks. Farther down the table Lachlan was bracketed on either side by Sister Collette and Sister Genevieve: the youngest nuns at the convent. If their laughter was any indication, they were enjoying the rare presence of a handsome young man in their midst.

Good humor and lively conversation abounded as Abbess Catherine set the meal in motion. Several of her fellow sisters brought forth serving trays laden with roasted chicken and vegetables. The smell of savory onions and rosemary permeated the frater as the nuns set the platters on each table.

After the blessing was said, the nuns and their guests started serving themselves. Yet Vivian had no stomach for food. She eyed the empty seat on the bench beside her. She should be glad of his absence, yet instead she felt hollow and alone. She was accustomed to being alone. Why did it bother her so much tonight?

"Never ye mind about his absence, m'lady," Gillis said from across the table. "He's no doubt preparin' fer our departure on the morrow. I'm sure there's much to oversee."

Moreis nodded his agreement. "The lad has much on his mind."

Vivian managed a half-hearted smile. "To be sure." Or was he merely avoiding her?

A murmur of noise brought her attention to the doorway as Quinn entered the chamber. He nodded as he passed the sisters who called out greetings to him, but he did not stop to engage them in conversation. Instead he headed straight for Vivian as though her thoughts had summoned him forth.

An exquisite rush of pleasure flooded her. He'd come to the banquet after all. And it appeared as though he had not only changed his traveling clothes for something far more elaborate, but he had also bathed. Damp tendrils of dark hair fell forward across his brow. He wore a crisp white linen shirt with a scarf tied about his neck. Covering his chest was a dark blue tunic embroidered with gold thread. Black trews encased his legs, revealing muscular thighs. He smelled good, too, fresh and clean with a hint of cloves.

"Forgive me for my lateness," he greeted as he slipped onto the bench beside her. "A bath seemed appropriate after battling Lachlan all afternoon."

Unable to pull her gaze away, Vivian nodded. The warrior of earlier was gone, replaced with the charm and refinement of a laird. She could not wrestle her gaze away from his clean-shaven cheeks or the sight of his damp hair as it curled against his muscular neck.

Vivian was suddenly grateful she had listened to Gillis earlier and had changed into the nicer of the two dresses she possessed. The gold-colored gown was simple with lace at the hem and sleeves. The bodice fit her to perfection, accentuating her curves. Gillis had rounded up two new ribbons, which she'd tied at her waist and her throat.

Quinn seemed to notice the new embellishments as his gaze shifted from her face, down the length of her neck, to her bosom, then waist, and back up again. A look of admiration reflected in his dark eyes. Any further conversation was interrupted as Sister Esther approached, bearing a platter of roasted chicken, turnips, and onions from which they were to serve themselves. A second tray followed, containing apple slices, cheese wedges, and fruit tarts.

Quinn filled her plate first, then his own. His interest shifted to the food before him. He took a bite of chicken. His eyes drifted closed as he chewed. "'Tis the best chicken I've ever tasted. Either the nuns are truly magnificent cooks or else I am famished from all the training today," he said between bites.

"Perhaps a little of both." Vivian studied him from beneath lowered lashes as he continued to eat his meal to the exclusion of all else, appearing more like a man who had gone days without food than a laird at a banquet. Tonight's meal was not nearly as splendid as the banquets she'd attended while at the king's court, but for the convent it was a rare luxury that no doubt stretched their meager resources. She would leave them one of the gemstones in the hem of her gown as payment.

Vivian returned her attention to her own food, picking at the meat with little interest until the man beside her leaned back with a contented sigh. His gaze dropped to her food.

He frowned. "Are you not hungry?"

"Nay. I suppose my mind is on other things." It wasn't a lie.

His expression grew somber. "You're upset that I cannot leave you here among the sisters."

"Nay. Doing so would put them all in danger if Rupert came looking for me."

"I'm glad we finally agree." He leaned toward her. His linen sleeve brushed her arm and her heart beat a little faster.

She shifted away, keeping space between them.

His brow furrowed. "'Tis best for everyone if we leave at first light."

"Then perhaps we should call it a night." She pushed back, preparing to stand.

He stalled her with a hand on hers. "The night is still young, and the sisters appear to have entertainment planned." He nodded to the four nuns who entered the frater just then, sending a sparkling refrain of music through the murmur of voices. A hush settled over the room as a dulcimer, a lute, a harp, and a drum chimed a steady beat. A cheer went up, and the long tables were pushed back, making room for dancers.

Two lines formed. The sisters joined in pairs. Lachlan was escorted by Sister Collette on one arm, and Sister Genevieve on the other. Even Gillis reached for Moreis, parading him into the fray. Vivian smiled as her foot started to tap to the beat.

"Dance with me, Vivian." Quinn held out his hand.

Her smile faltered. Giving in to the merriment with this man at her side was not a good idea.

"You do know how to dance, don't you?"

"Of course," she replied, tartly.

"Then let's show the others how it's done." Before she could object a second time, they stood and his arm encircled her waist as he guided her toward the ring of dancers.

Vivian's cheeks warmed as he sent her into a spin, making her feel as though she were floating on air. The room spun by in a whirl of colors. A swirl of air caused by the other dancers brushed her fevered cheeks.

It had been a long time since she'd let down her guard enough to enjoy a moment such as this. At King James's court she had hardly ever danced, fearful of letting anyone get too familiar with her. There was too much risk. But tonight, she allowed the rhythm of the music to move through her, washing away her inhibitions. She was surrounded by people she loved and trusted. She could indulge in such a folly one last time, could she not, before they departed into an unknown future?

Her excitement built. It was the result not only of the dance, but also of the way Quinn was looking at her, the way her blood pounded through her veins, the feel of her gown touching her flesh as she twisted and turned. The torches on the walls blurred into blue-orange flames before her eyes, and the thrum of the dulcimer and the beat of the drum echoed not only in her ears but her heart and her body.

Laughter bubbled up in her throat, and she felt almost too breathless to release it when all at once Quinn pulled her aside, out of the whirling throng and through the doorway of the frater. "What . . .?" She gazed up dizzily to see Quinn's face above hers. A slow warmth curled in Vivian's stomach, and the hollowness that always existed there seemed to vanish.

"One last indulgence." His pulse leapt at his temple. The look in his eyes was possessive. "I should not do this, but I find I cannot stop myself." His lips descended upon hers in a light kiss that left her yearning for more. His powerful body pressed her back against the stone wall and she could feel the tension of his muscles.

Her first real kiss. Dugald had only attempted a salute upon her cheek during their marriage, leaving her a virgin. And yet this man attempted already more than her husband of six months had. His tongue traced a hot line between her lips, coaxing them apart, then insisting. The moment she yielded, his tongue plunged inside, stroking and caressing.

She clutched at his shoulders as a wave of heat surged through her. She couldn't think. The drums, the music, the blood singing through her veins were all too loud, too powerful. She pulled back. "Someone will see us."

"They're all dancing." His lips pressed a kiss to her temples then her cheeks. "We are safe for the moment." He reclaimed her lips.

Quinn shouldn't be kissing her. Not when he'd said himself that his duty was to his brother and the king, yet instead of pulling away, she moaned with pleasure. Her mind was whirling as if she were still dancing, and her heart slammed against her rib cage. It was madness to give in to such abandon as though she were helpless in his arms.

But she wasn't helpless. She could fight him if she chose. Yet she knew with a sudden despair that she wouldn't fight him. Not tonight.

She murmured his name and closed her eyes and offered him her lips. The sweet offering of her mouth wrung a triumphant groan from him. He seized her lips in a kiss of melting hunger.

What was she doing? She didn't know this man—they'd only met days ago. And in that time, they had been besieged by constant threat. Perhaps it was because he'd played the role of her rescuer more than once. Was it gratitude she felt as his hand curved around her nape, sensually stroking it?

Nay, her mind objected with what small rational abilities she had left. This was something more—something bigger than both of them. He deepened his kiss. Raw pleasure streaked through her, and all she could do was surrender to the stormy splendor of the forbidden kiss. Her hands shifted restlessly over his heavily muscled shoulders and forearms, careful to avoid his injury. Her lips moved against his with increasing abandon, making her blood roar in her ears. Unable to stop herself, she arched against him, feeding his hunger and her own.

When finally he pulled his mouth from hers an eternity later, their breaths came in mingled gasps. Bereft of his touch, Vivian opened her eyes. His face was hard and dark with passion, his brown eyes smoldering. He lifted a hand to gently brush back a tendril of her hair from her cheek, and he tried to smile, but his breathing was as ragged as her own. "That was a bigger mistake than I feared it would be," he said on a tortured breath.

Vivian's swirling senses returned to reality. Slowly at first, then with a sickening plummet. Passion gave way to fear. She'd never felt anything so powerful in all her years. Closing her eyes, she fought the sting of tears that threatened. Confusion and anguish made her legs weak. Opening her eyes, she stepped back, out of his arms, then placed a hand against the wall to steady herself. "That was madness."

"Aye," he said, a raw edge to his voice. He stared at her with an intense stillness that made her realize Quinn Douglas was not a man to give in to innocent flirtations. He'd fought hard to stay away from this moment.

She scrambled backward, putting distance between them. "Why?" was all she could ask, her voice strangled. Why had he kissed her? Why had he shown her sensations she might never experience again?

"Inevitability?" Quinn said, the words filled with anguish.

Stunned by the panic rising within her, Vivian turned

and fled. She could not go back inside the frater and face Abbess Catherine, Sister Mary Margaret, Sister Agnes, or even Gillis. She had betrayed all of them with that one kiss. She'd betrayed the man who was supposed to be her husband. And she'd betrayed herself.

She raced out of the frater building, through the cloister, and back to her bedchamber. There, she shut the door behind her. She would go to sleep and not think of Quinn or the way his face had looked when he'd gazed into her eyes or the raw pleasure she'd experienced at his touch.

The fire in the brazier burned low and only the orange-red embers gave off light, casting the room in a faint glow. Vivian closed her eyes and leaned her cheek against the cold stone of the wall. Instantly, an image of Quinn appeared in her mind's eye. Vivian snapped her eyes open and drew a ragged breath.

She'd find no comfort in sleep when all her thoughts were of Quinn.

HE'D BEEN SUCH a fool to think that one kiss would ever be enough. Quinn curled his hands at his sides, fighting against the urge to go after Vivian—an urge so strong it was paralyzing his every thought and emotion. Against his better judgment he'd indulged in one kiss that he'd hoped would put the attraction he felt toward his brother's soon-to-be-wife to rest. One taste that would help him regain a sense of perspective for the duration of their trip to Redhouse Castle.

Instead, that one kiss had brought forth a need so overwhelming, a hunger so crippling, that he'd had to force himself to ease away from her before the smell, the taste, the feel of her undermined him completely.

She was to be his brother's wife. Quinn clenched his fists all the harder. He had to remember that fact for the next five days. Then he could hand Vivian over to Reid and hope that his brother realized the treasure he had been given by the king.

CHAPTER ELEVEN

RUPERT AND HIS men made their way through the forest outside of Tarbert. He reined his horse to a stop. The others followed.

"Where to now?" the man beside him asked.

"Straight ahead."

The dark-haired mercenary frowned. "Then why are we stopping? We picked up their trail. We should continue on before they escape."

"In time," Rupert replied, letting the man's insolence slide. Instead, Rupert filled his lungs with the cool, morning air, letting it slide through him, to heighten the slight pulse of excitement that nipped at his nerves.

He'd been anticipating Vivian's capture since yesterday afternoon when he'd picked up a trail through the forest that might very well be that of her and her traveling companions if four sets of hoofprints were any indication. He had dreamed of what he'd do to the girl all through the night. He'd awakened in a sweat at the thought of witnessing her pain. He needed her pain, her suffering. It was only when he inflicted pain on others or observed their raw emotions that he felt a surge of sensation in himself.

His mother had deadened him to all feeling with her failed attempt on his life. The bewitched image she'd used to torture him had left visible and invisible scars. The visible ones marked his chest. The invisible had dulled his nerves and his senses to the point he could hardly tell when he was injured in battle. Such a thing was a gift while fighting, but it left him feeling strangely dull most other times. Flat. Without the highs and lows he knew others experienced—the same sensations he sought now.

Rupert's muscles tautened as he leaned forward on his horse, his eyes narrowing on the outline of a buff-colored building in the distance. The witch was inside. She had to be.

He frowned at the realization that his quest would soon be at an end. 'Twas the drawback of hunting his prey. He always caught what he sought. Then he would have to begin anew.

Shrugging off the thought, Rupert focused on the here and now, on the attack that lay before him. His blood flared as it always did preceding the capture of a witch. Soon he would have his fun, soon he would experience the emotions he craved through her pain and eventual death.

"HOW LONG DO you estimate it will take us to reach

Redhouse Castle?" Vivian asked Lachlan the following morning outside the stable yard in an attempt at conversation. She waited near the barn while the men packed into the saddlebags the final supplies the nuns had offered for their journey.

The younger man shrugged. "Five days. Perhaps less, perhaps more, dependin' on how hard we push the horses and what trouble we find along the way."

Trouble in the form of Rupert and his men, no doubt. Vivian was at a loss for anything more to say. She was finding it very hard to keep her gaze away from the man packing Odin's saddlebag. Quinn had maintained his distance from her since they'd started their preparations to leave. And yet she repeatedly had the strange feeling that he was watching her. Once she'd allowed her gaze to stray to him. He had glanced up and merely nodded to her with cool civility.

"Are you feeling well?" Gillis asked as she came alongside her mistress to wait. The maid's worried gaze took in Vivian's flushed cheeks.

With a bright, artificial smile Vivian replied, "I've never been better." She'd had very little sleep last night as her thoughts continually returned to Quinn and the feel of his lips on hers. Just thinking about that moment now filled her with warmth.

"Sister Mary Margaret, Sister Agnes, and Abbess Catherine asked that you not leave before Lauds concludes and they might say farewell to you in person."

Vivian nodded. The nuns were at their morning prayers. She would delay the travelers' departure as long as possible in order to see the women who meant so much to her one last time.

It wasn't long before Vivian spotted Sister Agnes running toward them, her habit flapping and a distressed look on her face.

"What is it? What's wrong?" Vivian asked as the breathless nun came to a stop. Gillis hovered at her side.

Sister Agnes wrung her hands in dismay while she tried to catch her breath. "He's here."

"Who's here?" Vivian asked, her own anxiety growing.

"Rupert and five men," she replied with misery. "They've found you."

Suddenly the air seemed to vibrate with a sense of waiting menace. Vivian trembled but kept her chin firm. She would not give in to fear, not when so many lives were at stake. She spun to face Quinn. "There is a secret back gate I can use to escape. If Rupert and his men don't find me here they will continue their search and leave all of you alone."

The angles of his jaw were rigid. "You'll not go alone."

"I must." No matter how terrified the thought made her, she would do what was best for them all. "Rupert is—"

He took her by the shoulders and stared into her face. "No arguments."

He turned to the others. "To the horses." Quinn's hands

moved to her waist as he lifted her onto Odin's back. A moment later he slid behind her, wrapping his arms protectively around her. His warmth tempered the icy sense of doom that had crept inside her.

Sister Agnes waved them to follow her. "Be as silent as you can. Sister Mary Margaret has gone to greet them at the gate. She will stall for as long as possible, buying you some time to make your way to the Grampian Mountains and the Highlands." The rugged terrain would offer them protection but the journey would also be treacherous and possibly deadly at this time of year.

The riders stayed to the shadows cast by the early morning light until they reached the tall iron gate just beyond the bell tower. The wrought-iron fence looked impenetrable, yet Vivian knew it was not. She'd escaped the confines of convent life many times in her childhood through the secret gate in order to go searching for herbs amongst the foothills. It was the gate she and Sister Emmelia had taken that fateful afternoon.

The hidden exit would be her salvation this time around, and it was possible she would never see the convent or the sisters within again. With a lump in her throat, Vivian watched as Sister Agnes unlatched the gate, hidden in the intricate pattern of the iron, and swung it wide for the horses to exit.

As silently as possible, they made their way toward the hills. Sister Agnes followed on foot until they reached a field covered in gorse and lowland shrubs. There, the nun cut a gorse branch, sweeping it methodically back and forth across the trail in order to eliminate all evidence of their departure as she walked backward to the gate.

They continued on toward the mist-shrouded peaks of the Grampian Mountains and the forbidding glens and corries within. This part of Scotland had a history steeped in bloodshed and violence. It was a land of dark gods and druids, of legends and superstitions. Vivian shivered at the thought.

Quinn tightened his arms around her in response. "We are safe for now."

"How can you be certain?" Vivian whispered.

Quinn looked over his shoulder, back down the slope they'd just climbed. "We have the advantage of seeing them should they follow us. And Rupert and his men are nowhere in sight. I doubt he's mad enough to follow us here."

Vivian cast her gaze over the graduating grade and the darkest black chasms they'd woven their way through already. She turned back around, looking up at the twisted path before them. Drawing in a breath of the sweet mountain heather, she let it slide through her. They would be safe here in the mountains.

By midday they finally reached the top of the hill they'd been climbing. "Let's give the horses a rest," Quinn announced as he reined his horse to a stop. He dismounted before taking Vivian by the waist and helping her down. He released her quickly and returned his attention to his horse to remove the saddlebag. Once that task was complete, he hobbled the horses to the gorse branches near a patch of sweet deer grass to graze. From within the bag he dug out a parcel of bread and cheese, setting it on a nearby rock. "There's no better view than from right here." He patted a space on the rock beside him.

Vivian took a seat and her breath caught in her lungs. In the distance, the bluish mountains dominated the skyline and seemed to go on forever. In the foreground, the trail they'd been following suddenly seemed to end in a void of space. A ledge of rock marked the edge of the rim of a cliff that fell several hundred feet straight down. "How will we get down there?"

Quinn pointed to the left where a trail had been cut into the rock, looking more like a thin ribbon in the blue-green hillside than a navigable path. "The horses can make it. Never fear."

Her heart thrummed at the base of her throat with equal parts terror and awe. Instead of focusing on the path, Vivian looked beyond it to the sweeping russet meadows, the winding silver slashes of rivers and streams, the steep and craggy peaks that lost their summits in the shrouds of opaque mists before falling into the inky waters of the loch below.

"It's beautiful," she breathed.

"Beautiful, indeed," he agreed softly.

Something in his voice suggested his comment was not

directed entirely to the view. It was then she became aware that she had shifted closer to his side and into the protective circle of his arms. The sunlight played with the breeze-blown wisps of his hair, scattering them like threads of silk against the collar of his dark jacket. His eyes absorbed the color of the sky and shimmered with flecks of gold. He smelled like freshly cut grass and cloves, and the effect was intoxicating. It reacted with her senses, sending a ripple of pleasure across the surface of her skin.

In the silence that followed, Vivian heard a sound she'd missed before: the muted rushing of water. She used her sudden interest as an excuse to shift away. "Is that a waterfall I hear?"

"On your right," Quinn replied with a knowing smile. "There are many hidden falls in these hills."

Heat rushed to her cheeks as she stood and shifted toward the right, just enough to see a thin cascade of water tumbling through a fissure in the cliff, spraying a transparent mist onto the rocks below.

He watched her without further comment until finally Moreis cleared his throat and announced that it was time to eat, pointing to the blanket Gillis had set out farther back from the edge of the cliff.

The five of them sat down, enjoying the view as Gillis passed a platter of bread, cheese, and hard-boiled eggs. The conversation remained casual as they ate. When they were done Gillis and Moreis set about repacking their supplies while Lachlan tended the horses, leaving Quinn and Vivian alone once more. He helped her up and they walked back to the cliff's edge.

Abstractedly, Quinn stretched his injured arm.

"Are you still in pain?" Vivian asked. "I could fix you a tisane before we ride out again?"

He turned toward her. Sunlight glowed on his face and brought a sparkle to his eyes, drawing attention to the length of his lashes, the glossy thickness of his hair, even the roguish shadow of stubble on his jaw. "Nay. I need my senses sharp while we traverse the trail down."

"I can mix something for the pain that will not impair your abilities."

"Truly, I am well."

She gave a nervous laugh. "Forgive me. Old habits die hard. I did not mean to sound like your mother."

He stiffened. "Someone's mother maybe. Not mine."

"Why would you say that?" Curiosity burned inside her.

He shrugged. "She left Reid and me when we were infants. Twins were more work than she'd bargained for with my father always at war." He looked away, staring off into the distance.

A tight band constricted her breathing. She knew what it felt like to lose a parent to death, but not to desertion. "Do you have any memories of her?"

He turned back to face her, his face somber. "Only the ones I've created for myself."

He looked so vulnerable in that moment that Vivian couldn't help but take his hands in hers. A lump rose to her throat, making it impossible to speak even if she'd known what to say. She stared down at their entwined fingers, trying to think of something, anything to fill the silence.

"Do not despair. Reid and I had a happy childhood thanks to our stepmother."

Relief flooded her. "Do you have other siblings?"

"Aye. A younger half-sister, Evaline."

Vivian smiled. "Poor girl to have you twin brothers to torment her. I'm sure you teased her mercilessly."

"Nay," he replied with a chuckle. "It was Reid who teased her. I defended her."

"You said Reid is older?"

"By four minutes."

Vivian laughed but the sound faded away as he lifted their twined fingers to his cheek, pressing into her touch as though he needed the comfort she offered.

"Those four minutes made Reid the clan chief and the Earl of Douglas."

The warmth of his skin heated her own. Almost of their own volition, her fingers stroked his cheek and jaw. "Do you ever wish your birth order were reversed?"

"Nay, Reid is a born leader. He has guided the clan through times of war and peace."

"And what about you?"

He shrugged. "I'm an advocate for peace."

"Does a warrior long for peace?" she asked.

"When he's seen enough bloodshed and death, he longs to nurture life instead."

In the sunlight, the linen of his shirt was almost transparent, affording her a breathtaking reminder of the hard, sinuous muscles in his arms and across the breadth of his chest. He possessed a deadly grace and power as he had proven when she was attacked. He might long to be a farmer, but she knew even as such he would continue to fight for something or someone he believed in.

He had fought for her on more than one occasion.

"Vivian—" The warmth in Quinn's voice dragged her attention back to his face. "We're packed and ready to go."

She dropped her fingers from the warmth of his cheek and stepped back. "Of course," Vivian stammered as she moved to Odin's side, waiting for Quinn to lift her onto the saddle. A moment later Quinn mounted behind her.

"Ready?" he asked as they started toward the steep descent of the thin trail ahead.

"Nay," she replied honestly as they joined the others who were already mounted.

Quinn took the lead down the trail. His arms tightened around her.

Vivian drew what felt like a final breath as they started down, knowing she would not breathe easily again until they reached the valley below.

The descent from the bluff was hair-raising and slow.

Hours passed as Vivian resigned herself to bumping along on Odin's back. There was no relief from the uneven gait. She was so sore she almost begged to walk until she looked at the steep path ahead and changed her mind.

By sunset they left the mountainous part of the trail behind, entering the valley below. The temperature had fallen significantly as the sun dropped below the horizon, but Vivian hardly noticed as exhaustion held her in its grip.

A short time later Quinn brought Odin to a stop. "We'll make camp here on the shores of Loch Lomond. This trail is little known and even less used, so I think we can risk a fire." Quinn jumped to the ground then helped her dismount. He set her on her feet.

Her knees buckled for just a moment as blood flooded into her legs in painful pins and needles. "How can I help?" Vivian asked as the others started preparing the campsite.

"Do you cook?"

"Nay. At the convent the nuns cooked for me and at court the king had a complete staff in the kitchen. I never had the opportunity to learn anything other than how to create my healing concoctions," she replied as Lachlan took charge of the horses, stripping them of their heavy packs and removing their tack. Moreis gathered wood for a fire while Gillis set up their sleeping pallets.

"Then just rest. It's been a long day. I must help Lachlan with the horses. Will you be all right?"

She nodded and with a frown watched Quinn stride

away. Did he not think her capable of anything? Despite her agitation at watching the others work while she rested, Vivian looked for comfort in the quiet. No longer did she hear the constant clip-clop of the horses' feet against the trail or the rustling of the packs as they shifted back and forth.

Vivian closed her eyes and drew a deep breath, reveling in the evening air heavy with the sweet scent of heather. Slowly the sounds of the night revealed themselves. The hoot of an owl in the distance. The gentle lapping of the water against the shore. The rustle of the gorse leaves as the breeze tumbled through. A quiet splash of something in the loch.

Vivian opened her eyes. There *was* something she could do to help. With a renewed burst of energy, she slipped off her half boots and stockings and headed several yards down the embankment toward the shoreline. Hitching the hem of her dress into the waist of her skirt, she entered the water up to her knees and stood as still as possible, her hands hovering above the water.

"What are you doing?" Quinn asked from the shore.

Vivian turned around. "Shh. I'm fishing."

Shock mixed with amusement on Quinn's face. "With your hands?"

"Sister Mary Margaret taught me how. Now be quiet." Trying her best to ignore him, Vivian turned back around, concentrating on her task. A heartbeat later a sea trout swam between her legs. Quickly, she clasped her hands together and snagged the fish from the water. Within a few moments she had caught four more.

"You're very good at that," Quinn said, regarding her with curiosity as she waded back toward shore and the fish she'd thrown there.

"Since I caught them, you can clean them."

"Agreed."

She could feel the heat of his gaze on her bare legs. Hastily, she lowered her gown as warmth colored her cheeks. She bent to retrieve the fish when Quinn stopped her with a hand on her arm.

Gently he took her chin between his forefinger and thumb, tipping her face up to his. "Do you know what kind of torture today was for me? Holding you so close? The feel of your body, the scent of your hair, the warmth of your skin?"

"I—" she began, then stopped at the heated look in his eyes. He stepped closer and drew her against his chest with his other arm. He looked as if he wanted to kiss her.

Her gaze dropped to his finely molded lips, watching as a faint smile lifted the corners, and inch by inch he drew her closer.

She made no protest when he bent his head down. A shock jolted through her as his lips touched hers, warm and inviting, brushing slowly back and forth, teasing her. But when she leaned in to him, his hand left her chin to sensuously trace a line down her neck, across her shoulder and down the long line of her back.

Vivian slid her hands up the front of his shirt, feeling his muscles tauten. His mouth opened on hers, and Vivian felt her heart begin to beat faster as his tongue flicked against her lips, teasing her, inviting her, challenging her for more.

Sliding her hands around his shoulders, she kissed him back with a fierceness she hadn't known she possessed, drawing his tongue into her mouth. She felt his sharp intake of breath as desire surged in her own veins. Her soul stirred, longing for something she did not recognize. A slight breeze brushed her cheeks, bringing with it the familiar scent of heather from the hills beyond, seducing her every bit as much as the man in her arms.

He plunged his hands into her hair, pulling her fully against his hardening body, demanding more.

This second kiss was even better than the first. Stronger, wilder, as though they'd both denied themselves only to succumb to temptation in the end. To continue would be complete insanity, and yet she couldn't find the strength to pull out of his arms until a male voice suddenly erupted behind them.

"God's blood! What's goin' on here?"

Vivian jerked free in a panic at the sound of Moreis's voice.

"We were fishing," Quinn replied, his voice as deep and raw as she felt.

Moreis's surprised gaze flew from Vivian's flushed face to Quinn's ruffled hair. "Is that what they call it these days?"

His expression shifted to one of understanding. "Ye'd best come back tae camp before Gillis becomes even more overwrought. She's convinced herself that Rupert abducted ye."

Cringing with mortification, Vivian cast a glance at Quinn who regarded Moreis not with shame or regret, but with irritated amusement. Her cheeks flaming anew, she bent to retrieve two of the trout she'd caught while Quinn scooped up the remaining three. "We truly were fishing," she said as she fled back toward camp.

CHAPTER TWELVE

QUINN STARED INTO the fire, watching the steam rising from the fish he'd laid in the coals. His stomach growled at the fragrant, savory scent of the sea trout. He was so hungry the pain in his stomach kept his eyes from slamming shut in exhaustion.

He glanced at Vivian, sitting beside him. She leaned back against a tree, as exhausted as the rest of them. Yet as he studied her his heart jumped in his chest. Her hair had escaped its constraints and trailed carelessly over her shoulders like burnished copper. Her skin was pale, but against the deep green of the valley and blue-white hint of mist, she looked luminous, radiant.

He wondered what her reaction would be if she knew how often he'd dreamed about her during the past three days. How often he'd dreamed about touching her, caressing her, doing more than that . . . to his brother's bride.

He squeezed his eyes shut, chastising himself. What kind of man was he to want something so badly that was not his to take?

"Quinn?"

Her voice cut through his thoughts. He focused on the lilting sound, banishing all else, until he could almost feel the warmth of her skin beneath his hands. He curled his fingers into fists.

"You do not look well." She sounded uncertain, hesitant. Strangely breathless.

He was certain he would never be well again. "I am simply tired like everyone else." He opened his eyes and turned toward her.

"Oh." She shifted to stand. "Then I'll leave you alone—"

"Don't go." His hand covered hers, stalling her movements. He tensed, waiting for her refusal.

Moreis's gaze shot to the two of them, his bushy brows lifting. The older man stood near the fire while Gillis and Lachlan still milled around, preparing for the night ahead.

Vivian's cheeks flamed anew, no doubt remembering how they'd been discovered earlier by the lake. Quinn pulled his hand away. When Vivian settled back against the tree, relief spilled through him. "Would you like to know more about where we are headed?"

She nodded. "Is Redhouse Castle your family home?"

"Nay. Douglas Castle in South Lanarkshire is the family seat, but Reid prefers Redhouse Castle in North Berwick. It was given to Reid by King James."

"Bit of a shambles it is," Lachlan added as he came to join them at the fire. "The old place hasn't had a woman's touch for many a year. Long before the king gave it to Reid."

"Truly, it's not that bad," Quinn added when Vivian's face went pale. "Happily, the walls are impenetrable. Add to that the fact the fortification resides on the cliffs overlooking the Firth of Forth. The sea air is quite restorative for anything that might ail you in the future."

Quinn ignored the pain that squeezed his chest. Why was he trying so hard to convince her that Redhouse Castle was the place for her? He could see her more at ease in his own home in Dumfriesshire surrounded by the sweeping hillsides of the Scottish Lowlands.

"Do you live with your brother?" she asked, her voice thin.

"Yay and nay. When we are battling, I am at Redhouse, but most of the time I spend at my own estate miles away; Kinmount House."

Her blue eyes darkened. He saw the flash of something that looked like sadness—or regret—cross her face, but it was gone just as quickly. "Of course."

"Quit scaring the poor lass," Moreis said as he lumbered up to the fire and sat down. "Redhouse Castle is as fine a seat as any in Scotland. Ye'll be able tae put yer own mark on the place and make it yer home."

Vivian's lips were pressed into a thin white line as she stared into the fire. What Quinn wouldn't give to know her thoughts at the moment . . . but he dared not ask. Not in front of the others.

"Is that fish done yet?" Lachlan complained, breaking the

silence that had fallen over the camp.

"Smells done. Let me get that fer ye," Gillis said, moving toward the fire. She reached for a pile of tin bowls stacked nearby. Holding the metal bowls by the edge of her skirt, she dished up the steaming fish. Carefully, she passed the bowls to Lachlan, Moreis, and Quinn before serving Vivian and then herself.

Quinn's stomach growled even as he took his first bite of the mouth-watering fish. They ate in silence. The sounds around them seemed to intensify: the soft pad of animals in the bushes, frogs croaking near the loch, the hum and clicking of insects. All normal sounds of the night and nothing they had to fear.

As though sensing the direction of his thoughts, Vivian stopped eating and set her bowl aside. "Do you think Rupert and his men can have followed us here?"

"Nay," Quinn said with conviction. "No one unfamiliar with the descending path would dare, especially at night. Rupert is dangerous, but he's no fool."

"I agree," Moreis added. "We're safe fer now, but once we cross through Stirling toward Glasgow we had best be prepared."

"We can all sleep with ease tonight. The fire will keep the animals away." Lachlan stood then stretched with a yawn. "Now that my belly is full, I'm going to finally get some sleep."

Gillis joined him, gathering the now empty bowls. "I'll

clean the dishes in the loch then head to sleep myself."

Moreis stood and grabbed the dish beside Vivian to add to his own. "I'll help ye," he said. And, after giving Vivian and Quinn a speaking glance, he followed Gillis, leaving them alone.

Quinn's thoughts returned to their earlier conversation about Redhouse Castle. Vivian's body was still stiff and her face emotionless since their earlier discussion. "Are you upset that your new home will not be as grand as those you've lived in before?"

She turned toward him, eyes over bright. "Where I live matters not as long as I am happy."

"And do you imagine you can be happy in East Lothian with my brother?" His stomach clenched. Sudden tension made his shoulders tight. Not for the first time did he wish things could be different for both of them.

"I realize I am being unfair, for I haven't met your brother yet, but the closer we get to the end of our journey, the more fearful I become."

"Of Reid?" he asked.

She shook her head briefly. "Mostly of what could happen between now and our arrival, with Rupert . . . with those hunting me . . . the witch trials . . . with you."

He shoved his hands through his hair. "We are friends, Vivian. That's all we can be."

She lowered her gaze, shielding her response from him.

"Perhaps we should call it a night." He rose to his feet,

backing away from the fire. What in Hades was wrong with him? She had wanted something more from him tonight and he was walking away.

She is your brother's bride.

He reached out to grasp the trunk of a tree with one hand. His fingers dug at the bark until a ripple of pain went through him. He welcomed it as a distraction from another maddening ache.

"Good night then." Sorrow echoed in her tone. She was still for a moment before she stood and headed toward the loch.

Quinn stared after her. Even though he shouldn't, he wanted her. He wasn't sure at what point he had become aware he wanted her. That first day when he'd helped her to her feet after Odin had nearly trampled her?

Aye, he had wanted her then. His palm had tingled as it had touched the silky softness of her skin. Even then, he had tried to dismiss her effect upon him. He had to remember why he sought her and what his duty was. Yet never had his duty been this difficult to uphold.

Freed from the firelight, moonlight painted her in shades of silver and blue. As she walked she released the pins from her hair, allowing her long tresses to cascade down her back. The burnished-red locks shimmered as she walked. The sight of her made him want to reach out and—"Where are you going?"

She turned back toward him. "You said yourself we'd be

safe from Rupert tonight so I am going to bathe in the loch."

"Not by yourself, you're not."

"Moreis and Gillis are there. I will send Moreis back and keep Gillis with me." Vivian turned and left him, vanishing into the dark.

In all his years of warring alongside his brother, Quinn had always managed to shape events the way he wished them to go through strategy and diligence. And yet, where Vivian was concerned nothing had proceeded as planned.

They would spend four more days and nights together. They would no doubt be the four most torturous of his life.

CHAPTER THIRTEEN

VIVIAN GROANED AS she slid from Odin's back the next evening. Sore and tired, she was grateful for the reprieve. After a treacherous day spent making their way through the hills and valleys of the lowlands, they had reached the outskirts of Glasgow just as the clouds overhead threatened rain. They set up camp inside a large cave in the hillside overlooking a river. Caves always made Vivian a little nervous because of the darkness, but Quinn had convinced her the natural structure was their best hope for both shelter from the storm and protection from Rupert if he were searching the area.

Once the horses were settled inside the cave, Quinn gave orders to the others to get their campsite set up before the gray clouds overhead released their promise of rain. Wanting to contribute, Vivian set about gathering wood for a fire. As she did, she scanned the area, looking and listening for any signs of Rupert and his men.

Now that the travelers no longer had the protection of the steep cliffs and impenetrable valleys to hide them, they had to be extremely careful. Here in the foothills they were exposed and would remain that way over the next three days of travel. Quinn was driving them hard, but with good reason. Danger could be anywhere.

Forcing her anxiety aside, Vivian continued to pick up whatever she could find that would burn. Fire in the cave would ease her fear and also keep them warm while they slept. She paused for a moment to watch a gray heron as it fished in the river curling at the bottom of the bank below her. Perhaps when she had completed her task she would try her hand at fishing again.

The image of the bird suddenly faltered, and a telltale pain pulsed behind her eyes. As another vision crashed through her brain, her booted feet skidded on the moss beneath her. She struggled to stay in the here and now as the wood flew out of her hands and she went sliding. Roots, rocks, and sharp-edged gorse branches clawed at her skin and dress as she tumbled. She flailed out, desperately seeking something, anything to halt her downward plunge toward the river, but she was moving too fast.

From behind her, she heard Quinn shouting. She couldn't make sense of the words as the pounding at her temples increased. She cried out in pain and shock as she hit the icy water and plunged below the surface.

This was how Sister Emmelia had died. Perhaps it was justice that she, too, suffer a similar fate. The river's current caught Vivian, but instead of pulling her under, she seemed to be floating as the vision she'd tried to fight took hold.

Late afternoon, and yet a full moon hung swollen and glistening in the sky. In a room that was whole, but also in ruin. A man stood beside a lone woman. He, dressed in an elegant green coat trimmed in gold brocade with black knee breeches. The woman, with alabaster hair and wearing a tattered white dress. She hung her head, defeated, refusing to look at the man.

Moonlight shifted. This was no ordinary man, but King James, her guardian at a witch's tribunal.

Her head dipped below the surface of the river and her dress tugged her down. Air and water, two worlds, like the one her body was in, and the one that stole her mind. Pressure built in her chest, threatening to break free. She flailed, and broke through the surface, gasping for a breath even as the water and her vision dragged her back under.

Pain throbbed behind her eyes. *King James questioning the sobbing young woman. Another shadow detached itself from the gathered crowd. A flash of metal. A fierce rush of anger. The unknown assailant dashed forward, his knife poised to strike.*

Terror shot through Vivian as she watched the king fall to the ground. He died as he had always feared—at the hands of a madman. She watched as his breathing stopped and life fluttered from behind his eyes.

Vivian's body went limp as exhaustion from fighting the water and her vision drained her. Why would she have this vision now, when she was unable to do anything to stop the inevitable from happening?

"Nay!"

A deep-voiced cry of despair rent the air, pulling her back

to the moment. Through the churning water, Vivian's gaze moved to the water's edge. Quinn raced along the riverbank, chasing her. She tried to raise her hand, but she did not have the strength. The vision had taken its usual toll and a cold numbness permeated her limbs.

"Vivian!"

Dimly she heard the sound of splashing as she bobbed above then below the surface of the churning water. The water clawed at her, pulled her away from air, away from life.

Then a vise grasped her, yanked her up. She could hear Quinn's harsh breathing beside her. He repositioned her in the cradle of his arms and trudged through the water toward the riverbank.

At the water's edge, he sank to the ground with her still in his arms. His breathing was labored. "You—scared me."

Vivian looked up. His complexion had gone white. His dark hair clung to his face, sending rivulets of water down his cheeks.

"I pushed us all too hard today, I'm sorry," he said as the fear in his eyes faded.

She looked up at him, trying to steady the trembling in her fingers, the quick, loud pounding of her heart. His eyes were dark. There was some emotion in them, something she couldn't name, something uncertain and filled with yearning. It pulled at her, pierced her heart, made her feel warm and icy cold at the same time.

He leaned toward her. "I could have lost you—"

"Vivian!" Gillis came rushing up. Worry lines bracketed her eyes and mouth. "Are you hurt?"

"I don't think so."

"You could have drowned." Gillis's gaze dropped to the hem of Vivian's gown and sharpened there.

Vivian startled. Her maid saw the proof of a secret: that she'd hidden her gemstones, funded by the items her patients had given her, now partially visible through the hem of her sodden gown. Secreting them had been the only way to make certain her treasures remained her own in the future.

"Do you think you can stand?" Quinn asked when his breathing returned to normal.

She nodded.

"Thank you," she said to Quinn, grateful he did not seem to notice the hem of her gown.

"No thanks are required." His arms remained around her, but she could feel him withdraw both physically and emotionally. "'Tis my duty to help you."

Vivian felt a stab of regret as Quinn assisted her to her feet.

Gillis slipped between the two of them and wrapped an arm around Vivian's shoulders. "We need to get you back to camp."

Over her shoulder Vivian turned to look at Quinn. He stood by the riverbank, unmoving. His eyes were trained on her as she walked away. A desperate sadness reflected there. One that echoed in her own soul. Her throat tightened as the tears she refused to let fall burned at the back of her eyes. Tears for herself. Tears for the king. Tears for them all.

Then, as if the sky would do what she would not, it started to rain.

THE RAIN FELL in sheets around them, making the twilight sky seem darker than it was. By the time Quinn returned to the cave, Moreis and Lachlan had a fire going, and the savory smell of stew floated through the camp. Quinn sank down on a blanket near the fire to warm himself. He could hear Vivian's quiet breathing beside him, mixing with the crackling snap of the fire. In the semidarkness, they were comforting sounds.

Gillis had helped Vivian out of her sodden garments and into her other dress. Moreis and Lachlan lay on blankets on the opposite side of the fire, warming themselves as they awaited their evening meal. Gillis tended the rabbit stew. She stirred the pot's contents, filling the air with a mouthwatering smell before she turned away to prepare the serving bowls.

Quinn stared into the fire, watching steam from the stew rise into the air. His stomach growled at the fragrant scent of meat, carrots, parsnips, and onions. In spite of the delicious meal that awaited them and the warmth they all enjoyed, he hated that they'd had to build a fire. He worried the smoke might alert Rupert to their location.

When he could avoid looking at her no longer, Quinn glanced at Vivian. Though she was dry, her hair was still tangled and loose and fell in her face.

She shivered.

Remorse that he hadn't thought to warm her earlier flashed through him. Quinn reached behind him for a second blanket and wrapped it around her shoulders. "For the chill."

She shivered again. "Thank you."

Her blue eyes showed sadness and a hint of fear. They also reflected determination. Longing to lighten her mood, Quinn reached toward her, tucking a yet damp lock of hair behind her ear. "I could plait your hair for you, if you'd like. That would at least get the wetness off your skin."

She startled at the offer. "I don't think that would be wise."

"Nay?" he replied with a shrug. "My sister forced me to plait her hair when she was younger. I'm quite good at it."

"Your sister preferred plaits to curls?"

Quinn chuckled at the memory of his sister. "Evaline has always been on the spirited side. She didn't like anything that got in her way. Not her hair, and definitely not her brothers."

Vivian smiled and the sadness in her eyes vanished. "She sounds like someone I'd like to meet."

Quinn's mood sobered. "You will meet her once we

reach Redhouse Castle."

Silence settled over the cave until Vivian finally asked, "You really know how to plait?"

"Try me."

She finally nodded.

He shifted behind her and began to comb his fingers through her damp hair. She stiffened at this touch, but he didn't stop. Instead, he gathered the long tresses in his hands and pushed his fingers through her hair. Her hair felt like satin. Heavy dark satin, winding through his fingers like a burst of red firelight.

At the thought, a lick of fire tickled his veins, and a shudder of awareness slid through him. He clenched his jaw, fighting the urge to bury himself in her tresses, tormenting himself with the thought of wrapping the thick softness around him.

He'd barely touched her, yet he suddenly wanted her so badly he could barely draw breath. Steeling himself, he dropped her hair against her back and laid the strands flat in preparation for plaiting.

What was he doing? The desire to kiss her was almost overwhelming. It was a good thing the others were present. They were the deterrent he needed to plait her hair without touching her more. Drawing a deep breath to focus his thoughts, he skillfully moved his fingers through her hair, starting at the crown of her head all the way down her back. When he reached the end, he tied it off with the ribbon she'd worn around her neck at the convent, then released her.

She shifted back to face him and tossed the length of the plait over her shoulder. His gaze lingered on the silken strands that caressed her neck. He curled his fingers into fists. Despite any thoughts of control, truth was he wanted to kiss her, to make love to her.

Heat curled in his stomach. He closed his eyes for a moment, swallowing back his desire, wishing his emotions weren't so close to the edge. All he had to do was look at her and he was hard, ready, wanting something he had no right to take.

And still he longed for the forbidden.

In an effort to clear his head, Quinn reclined on the blanket beneath him. He'd never had such unchivalrous thoughts in his whole life. He'd agreed to perform this service for his brother in the hopes of curtailing Reid's lust for excitement and danger. And although he'd intended the retrieval of his brother's bride to be quick and easy, the task was turning into the biggest challenge of Quinn's life. Because despite his sense of duty and honor to his brother, Quinn wanted Vivian as his own.

He opened his eyes to find her staring down at him. Her lips parted. Her breathing quickened. The air between them all but crackled. He wanted to touch her even with the others present. He curled his hands at his sides, fighting the urge.

As though sensing the direction of his thoughts, Vivian drew a deeper breath, then suddenly all color drained from her face.

In an instant Quinn sat up. "Vivian, what is it? What's wrong?"

SHE WAS IN a cave, or a shelter of some sort. There the ever-changing brilliance of a small fire. Quinn stretched out on a blanket. She sensed every action of his body: the rise and fall of his chest as he breathed. The tension in his hand as it gripped the blanket. The slight hollow beneath the bones of his cheeks as his lips tightened. And his eyes . . . they looked at her with desire.

The scent of rain. Earth. Burning wood; the scents surrounded them. She wanted to breathe in the aroma, and his scents, to gather them inside her senses, to remember them forever.

The sensual thought rippled through Vivian's senses as she recalled every moment of her previous vision and the one that had followed on its heels: the one detailing her own death by burning at the stake. Vivian drew a sharp breath, struggling for composure. Would she die before she ever had a chance to live? If what she had experienced only a heartbeat ago had come to pass with Quinn, then the second portion of that vision might also.

"Vivian, what's wrong?" Quinn had moved to his knees

in front of her. He wrapped his warm fingers around her icy ones. His eyes looked bottomless in the darkness, full of compassion and yearning. It was a look that begged her to tell him the truth about her visions.

A part of her longed to tell him. The burden of her visions was becoming difficult to carry alone. And yet two people she trusted and admired had warned her to keep that burden to herself. In these "burning times" she knew the risk of exposing her secret.

He had not turned on her when the villagers had called her a witch. He had not pushed her for an explanation when she knew they would be attacked. Even now, his expression was that of concern rather than anything forceful or demanding. Images of Quinn rushing to her aid when they were attacked and again when she was captured played across her mind. He'd comforted her when she was frightened. He'd warmed her when she was cold. He'd plaited her hair. How many men would do such a thing?

Quinn was strong without being domineering, gentle and kind and so unlike her father. The warrior before her had offered her a hundred little kindnesses on this journey, and she repaid him with a lack of trust.

With an agonized groan, Vivian pulled away, wrapping her hands in her skirt. "It's been an exhausting day." She got to her feet and moved to help Gillis serve the meal.

Across the fire, Quinn watched her every movement with a mixture of confusion and sorrow, bringing a dull throb of regret to her heart. Loneliness swept over her so intense she hugged her waist, digging her fingers into the fabric of her gown. She was tired of always being alone, excluding herself because of her secret. But if she wanted something different than the simple companionship they shared at present, she would have to tell him the truth.

CHAPTER FOURTEEN

THE FOLLOWING MORNING they made their way on horseback through the rugged terrain just east of Loch Lomond known as the Trossachs. The rain had lifted, replaced by a mist that crept across the valley. Despite her withdrawal from Quinn last night, he held her in his arms atop Odin as though nothing had transpired, bringing an unfamiliar warmth to settle in her belly as she watched the scenery go by.

Looming above the scenic valley were several cobblers and munros with the larger mountains of Ben A'an to the north and Ben Venue to the south. The area was heavily forested, and Quinn had chosen the route along the southern shores of Loch Katrine so they would have the cover of the trees to conceal them as they made their way through Stirlingshire. A sea of green stretched out before them, broken here and there by burgeoning waterfalls—swollen from the rain—that snuggled into the hillsides.

Quinn remained silent. When she turned to face him, he sent her a soft smile that made her feel . . . miserable.

Vivian's heart ached. "Why are you so kind to me?"

He pulled her closer, so close she could feel his heat. "It's my duty."

"Nay. It is not," she objected. "Why?"

Quinn was thoughtful a moment before replying, "We are friends. That's what friends do for each other."

His words swept over her, sank into her. "I'm not who you think I am."

"You aren't?" he asked, his tone light. "Who are you then?" The late morning sun lit his face, gilded his hair as he waited for her reply.

She had to tell him the truth. Vivian looked away, toward the trees. "I care about you," she said, her voice dropping to a whisper. "We are friends, and as your friend I don't want to disappoint you."

"Nothing you say or do will ever disappoint me."

His voice ran over her, deep and compelling, shivering along her spine and up the back of her neck until she turned her face back to his.

Vivian opened her mouth to speak just as a throbbing came to her temples. Slow thudding hit behind her eyes and at the back of her skull with mallet-hard force. A vision was coming. She winced at the pain. The image of Quinn wavered before her, until suddenly she was lost to the inevitable.

She was running. Her feet stumbling on the uneven ground. Then she was in a field of heather, still running. Panic rising within her. Moving deeper into the forest, toward the craggy hills. Branches lashed her face and clawed at her arms as she pushed herself to move faster.

Above her, the first stars burst into the night sky. The moon, three-quarters full, casting dappled shadows in the hazy darkness. Behind her, hoofbeats mixed with angry shouts.

"Stop!"

A sudden chill gripped her and she glanced over her shoulder.

Rupert thrashed through the underbrush atop his tall red horse, his sword drawn. Five men rode beside him. "You cannot outrun me, Witch."

The sound of hoofbeats growing closer. Vivian ran faster, trying to outdistance the man she feared more than any other. Jumping over a rock. Staggering. Almost falling, but a strong arm coming out to steady her. She did not run alone. Quinn, Moreis, Lachlan, and Gillis were beside her.

A surge of primitive satisfaction. She would not fall or die without gazing upon Quinn's face one last time.

Her satisfaction was short-lived. She stumbled to a halt. A solid wall of rock. She twisted around, desperately seeking a means of escape. They couldn't go around the wall. They couldn't go back toward Rupert and his men.

Trapped. Her stomach roiled and bile rushed her throat as she pressed back against the cold, wet rock.

"We must turn and fight." Quinn drew his sword. Beside him Moreis and Lachlan did the same. Tears streamed down Gillis's cheeks.

Hoofbeats grew louder. The Witch Hunter was almost upon

them.

They were all going to die!

Rage erupted inside Vivian. She slammed her hands against the rock. Fury formed. She would not be defenseless when Rupert arrived. Her anger would be her weapon. The ground trembled. A door lifted. She spun and fell backward into the wall of rock.

She stared up in stunned amazement at the tunnel that extended deep within the hillside. Cool darkness pressed in on her, stealing her breath. A sanctuary? Or a trap?

A wave of nausea tickled her stomach, then punched it as Vivian returned to the here and now. The rapid-fire beat of her heart thudded in her ears, pulsed at her temples. She brought her shaking fingers to her forehead, trying to hold back the pain.

"Vivian? What just happened to you?" he asked, the concern so strong in his voice it tugged painfully at her heart.

The last of her reservations faded away as deep inside she knew she could trust him. "I must speak with you. Alone."

Quinn nodded, then rode beside Moreis and Lachlan, instructing them to ride ahead and set up camp for the night. "We will join you soon."

"Everything all right?" Moreis asked, his brows drawing together with worry as he shifted his gaze to Vivian.

"All is well," Quinn reassured his friend. "We will only be a moment."

Gillis remained silent but Vivian could see the trepidation in her eyes.

"As you wish," Moreis responded as he led the others

away.

When they were alone, Quinn turned to Vivian. "Now tell me what is happening to you."

Vivian slid from the horse. Her knees buckled beneath her and she sagged to the moss-covered ground. The forest before her tilted, spun, became a frightening blur of brown and green.

Quinn was beside her. He took her trembling hands in his. "I can accept anything. But no more lies." His fingers threaded hers and closed tight, giving her an anchor as the forest continued to sway before her. He pulled her close, wrapping her in his heat. She closed her eyes and buried her face in his shoulder.

She didn't know how long she remained there, cradled by Quinn, but it seemed like forever. Gradually her strength returned and her headache diminished. Even the shaking in her fingers melted away.

Finally, Quinn pulled back and took her face in his hands, holding her as if she were made of the finest porcelain. "What has scared you so badly?"

A soft breeze whistled through the treetops above their heads, pulling the last of the vision's effects from her. Vivian drew a breath even as fear tumbled through her and said, "If we stay the course we are on, Rupert will attack tomorrow night when the moon is three-quarters full."

Quinn's dark eyes searched hers as his hands left her face to twine with her fingers once more. "How can you know that?"

She searched his face. The look in Quinn's eyes was not one of fear or judgment. Instead she saw compassion and understanding. He looked at her as if he knew what it felt like to have a secret so great it held you apart from everyone else, making you feel lost, and alone, and utterly afraid. In that moment she knew she could trust Quinn with her secret. "I . . . I see things . . . things in the future."

He looked at her not with fear and revulsion, but acceptance. "I suspected something was different about you." His brows drew together and his features became thoughtful. "That's why you knew those ruffians would attack us when we left Kilkerran?"

She nodded. "And how I knew that little boy would be trampled if I did not intervene."

"Do the things you see always happen?"

Images of last night, of Quinn reclining on the blanket in the cave, tumbled through her mind. Then just as quickly the image of Sister Emmelia's lifeless eyes stared up at her. Vivian shuddered at the memory. "Aye and nay," she replied honestly. "Mostly things happen as I see them. Once I tried to change what I'd seen by doing something at a different time and in a different way, but something worse happened as a result. I've never tried to change one of my visions again . . . and yet, I have been successful at allowing the vision to proceed and then changing some small part."

"So, you can alter the outcome?"

She shrugged. "The events still happened, but what transpires is ultimately different than what I have seen. I lost a friend—Emmelia. After Emmelia died, I've been frightened to do anything more."

"Then we have a chance to manipulate what you've seen about Rupert," Quinn said with determination in his voice.

That determination spilled over to her, as suddenly for the first time in a long while relief and hope filled her. Was there a chance to escape Rupert tomorrow night? Might she yet avoid her fate of burning at the stake? Could she save King James from a stabbing death? She had no way of knowing unless they put that theory to the test.

Smiling, she threw her arms around Quinn and hugged him.

He tensed at first then relaxed into her body. "What's that for?"

She swallowed the lump in her throat before pulling back to look at him. "For giving me hope."

He returned her smile. "Tell me what you have seen and we'll plan accordingly. Together, we can find a way to alter that fate."

For a moment, her joy wavered as fear once again crept inside her. What if she could only change a little bit of what she saw? What if she could spare the others but she still came to a fiery end at Rupert's hand? Her hands started to shake.

"What is it?" Quinn asked, his smile fading as he noticed the sudden change in her mood.

Her heart felt like it stopped beating. "What if what happened with Emmelia happens again?"

"We must try," Quinn said softly. "Remember, you're not alone on this journey."

She drew a harsh breath. "That's just it. Perhaps I should be. In order to avoid disaster, we must proceed with the journey as I have seen it. Then, to alter what happens, we must split up with you all going one way and me going another. Alone."

"Nay," Quinn said. "We've come this far together. I won't let you go back to being alone."

Their gazes locked; his unblinking and filled with confidence, hers afraid and yet filled with a profound sense of relief. "If you're certain you want to take that chance."

"I am. It is my duty and my honor to keep you safe."

Vivian frowned. She was starting to dislike those words. "How very chivalrous of you."

His mouth twitched. "Now tell me about your visions."

The man before her had a calmness at his center, a focus she was certain made him a deadly opponent. If anyone could take on Rupert and his men and win, it was Quinn. Bolstered by the thought, she told him every vision she'd had lately except the one of him in the cave and of her own death at the stake. Those she kept to herself.

When she was done, he asked, "Is that all of them?"

Vivian bit her lip. "Aye."

He was thoughtful for a moment before he said, "I want

to ride back to the ridge we just passed. Are you up for that?"

"You want to see if there are any signs of Rupert." She didn't blame him for wanting proof of what she had revealed.

"We might be able to determine how much of a lead we have on him and his men." He shrugged. "There might be nothing we can see from this distance, but it's worth checking out."

"I agree." She stood and allowed him to return her to Odin's back.

As they reached the ridge, no words passed between them. They scoured the area for signs of Rupert's presence. When she saw a slim column of smoke above the trees in the distance she knew Quinn had seen it as well by the sudden tension in his body.

"A campfire?" she asked.

Quinn nodded. "You were right. Rupert or someone is near. About a quarter of a day's ride away. We should be safe enough tonight, but we will need to put whatever plan of action we come up with into play before dawn if we are to stay ahead of them."

Quinn turned Odin back to the forest. "Let's rejoin the others. I need time to think about how best to proceed."

The flat, hard tone of his voice made it clear he was already considering his options. That he wouldn't rush into a new scheme left her feeling a little more steady. "Are you ready for what comes next?" he asked.

She faced him. "Aye. As long as whatever we do, we do together." Since he refused to allow her to face Rupert alone, then she would do all she could to see that he came to no harm. The thought of him suffering on her behalf made her physically ache.

His gaze held hers in a way that made her heart skitter a little. "Is it time to tell the others about your visions? Moreis and Lachlan will never agree to changing our plans unless they know about the danger ahead."

Gathering up her courage, Vivian nodded. "I'll tell them."

Quinn leaned forward and touched his forehead to hers, very softly, then backed away. "It's going to be all right, Vivian." Saying nothing more, he straightened and spurred Odin back toward the path the others had taken. When she settled against him, he tugged her a little closer, holding her that way until they arrived at the campsite. Quinn brought Odin to a stop then helped her dismount before doing the same. He handed Odin over to Lachlan who took the tired animal to join the other horses.

Gillis looked up from her place by the fire where she prepared their evening meal. "Come warm yerself, m'lady."

Vivian drifted toward the campfire and Gillis. The heat of the flames reached out to Vivian and gave her something to focus on while she mentally prepared herself for telling them all about her visions. She suspected Gillis already knew, but to Lachlan and Moreis the reality of her gift might come as a surprise.

As soon as Lachlan joined the men, they took places around the fire. Quinn sent her a reassuring smile before proceeding. "Vivian has something to discuss with you all."

Vivian squared her shoulders as all eyes turned to her. "The reason Rupert is pursing me is because he thinks I'm a witch."

"We knew that, milady," Lachlan said. "That's why we are taking you to safety at Redhouse Castle."

"What you don't know is that while I am no witch, I do possess certain abilities . . . more than simply healing people. I see things. Things in the future." She paused to let her words sink in. "I had a vision of our future if we stay our present course—one that leads to our deaths. Rupert and five of his men are in pursuit."

Moreis's features hardened. Before he could comment Quinn said, "Vivian and I backtracked to the ridge and verified that Rupert is not far from here. He and his men have settled for the night as we have, but we'll need a new way forward before dawn if we are to outmaneuver him."

Lachlan straightened. "The three of us can take on Rupert and his men. We've succeeded in similar situations before."

"Not with women to protect among us," Quinn replied. "There are too many variables, too many things that could go wrong. Our best option is to separate. Vivian's vision revealed a secret cavern. Lachlan, Vivian, and I will travel to the cavern then you, Lachlan, will break off and go to our brother-in-arms, Malcolm, while Vivian and I draw Rupert away from you."

Concern etched lines around Lachlan's eyes. "I realize Malcolm Hamilton and the Hamilton clan are in Falkirk not far from here, but I'll not leave you in such a predicament, alone."

"You must. The cavern Vivian saw will keep us safe until you return with reinforcements." Quinn released a slow, uneasy breath. "I've tried to keep others from this battle. The threat of retribution against anyone who crosses Rupert is great." Quinn's gaze passed between Lachlan and Moreis. "We can no longer avoid the fact that we need other members of the 'seven' to help us. We swore an oath to protect the king but also each other. It's time to ask for help."

"What about Gillis and me?" Moreis asked. "What is our part in all of this?"

"You will head to Redhouse Castle and bring back my brother and his army."

"Nay," Gillis argued. "If Vivian's vision has shown ye an unwinnable situation, then ye should run. Avoid the outcome altogether by heading back tae the Highlands. Wait fer the Lairds Hamilton and Douglas there."

Vivian shook her head. "Avoiding the situation is not the answer. I've tried that before. If at least some part of this vision does not hold true, then something with even more dire consequences will occur. Trust me on this."

"At least we all know what we are up against thanks to Vivian's insight," Quinn added.

"I won't go," Gillis objected, crossing her arms over her chest.

"You must go, Gillis. Do this for me."

Fear etched into the lines on Gillis's face. "Ye dinna understand. I can't leave ye. What if ye're captured?"

"I will protect her," Quinn said with determination. "You must go for our plan to succeed."

"Nay—"

"You are not the only one who cares for her, Gillis." Quinn's voice was infinitely soft.

The words defeated Gillis. Her shoulders slumped and she nodded slowly. "As ye wish. I'll go with Moreis, but know that I vow tae return, no matter the cost tae myself, should ye need me, m'lady."

"Thank you for your loyalty, Gillis," Vivian said humbly. A somber mood fell over the camp as they ate supper and prepared their sleeping rolls for the night. As the fire died down, silence fell over the campsite.

Unable to calm the thoughts racing through her mind, Vivian stared into the darkness for what felt like hours. It had been a long day, and emotionally draining, and yet she still could not sleep. Knowing the future did not make it any easier to embrace what was coming. With a soft sigh, she nestled deeper into her blanket and tried to think of other things.

Moreis and Lachlan snored softly on the other side of the

now extinguished fire. Gillis slept on Vivian's right side, her breathing slow and regular. Quinn slept on her left. Vivian took comfort in the sound of his soft, even breathing. Something subtle had shifted between herself and Quinn since the other night when he had plaited her hair. He no longer saw her as his brother's prize—something to be protected and held apart—but as a friend.

The thought brought a smile to her lips.

"Are you awake?" Quinn whispered.

"Aye," she replied, a thrill of anticipation moving through her. She turned toward him. In the shadows of the night she couldn't make out anything more than his shape, yet there was contentment in even that.

Silence settled over them for a long moment before she heard him shift closer. She could make out his features now in soft grayish hues. He reached for the long end of her plait, winding the end around his fingers.

Her breath caught. "What are you doing?"

"Touching you. Is that all right?"

She heard the pounding of her heart in the silence. He was so close she could feel his heat, smell the soft musk of his skin. "I suppose," she said, trying to control the tremble in her voice.

Absently, he continued to stroke her hair. "Can I ask you something?"

"Anything." She tried to see the expression on his face but could only make out the black shadow of his hair falling against his forehead.

"Did the king ask you to have visions on his behalf?"

"He asked, but my insight into the future doesn't work that way. It is never forced." She tried to keep her voice even, though tension suddenly filled her. "I have been able to meditate on a person, or a situation, and have some insight come to me about them in the form of a vision." Would he ask her to predict the future like the king or her late husband? Would he use her abilities in that way?

She swallowed, wishing she could see Quinn's expression now more than ever. She wanted to see if the eagerness that often lit the king's eyes at such a request was there in Quinn's. Or did she? "Why do you ask?"

Silence. Just when she thought he wouldn't answer, he said, "I was thinking about Reid. He is hunting the Earl of Bothwell."

Vivian's stomach clenched. "Do you want me to tell you if Reid finds the earl? Or where he can be found?"

"Nay!" Quinn's fingers stilled on her hair as he levered up on his elbow. "I would never ask that of you. I see the toll your visions take on you and the effects they leave behind."

Vivian stared at his shadow, stunned. "Then why ask me about my abilities?"

His sigh was heavy in the darkness. "My thoughts were jumbled, and I apologize if my words upset you. I was merely curious about your gift, and at the same time wondering if Reid will have returned to Redhouse Castle by the time we arrive. The two thoughts really had nothing to do with each other."

"We are both tired," she said, offering him an explanation.

"That's no excuse," he said as he edged closer. "I promise to never use your talents for my own gain, or for the advantage of others." His voice dipped, deepened. "Share your visions with me if you need someone to talk with about them, but only if you wish to."

Vivian felt something tickle her stomach, then warm, filling a space that was often hollow and bereft inside her. She tried to hold it back, but it erupted in a flood of sensation until she couldn't hold it back any longer.

He'd made a promise to her that no one had ever made before: to not use her abilities for his own gain. She smiled into the darkness. Vivian couldn't see his face, but somehow, she knew he smiled in return. Reaching for his fingers, she curled hers around his large ones. He returned the gentle squeeze, sending a shiver of pure happiness down her spine.

It had been a long while since she'd felt like this, content in her situation, even though she knew it was temporary at best.

Tomorrow, and all its foreseen troubles, would arrive before either of them wanted it to.

QUINN LAY AWAKE, watching Vivian sleep because he could

do nothing else. *Please, God,* he prayed. Let tomorrow work out as they had planned. Let the secret cavern shelter him and Vivian while the others escaped and went to find help. God didn't often answer his prayers, but that did not stop him from asking yet again.

Squeezing his eyes shut, Quinn tried to quell the fear welling inside him. He wasn't afraid of Rupert. Quinn had battled misguided men like Rupert and his henchmen before and triumphed by separating them into smaller groups that he could successfully battle alone. And battling the men alone would be a last resort—something he'd have to do if Malcolm Hamilton and his clan failed to arrive in time.

Yet it was more than Rupert and his men that troubled Quinn tonight. The last few days with Vivian, despite their troubles, had been the happiest days of his life. Once this final battle with Rupert was over, Quinn would have no choice but to deliver the woman he'd grown to care about to his brother.

Reid would care for Vivian. He would see all her needs were met. But would he love her? Would he respect her gift? Or would he try to use her as others had?

Both temper and desolation welled up inside him. Reid might very well extort her visions for his own gain. His brother often took what he wanted in order to further his own ambitions. Could Quinn allow that, or was a new battle brewing? One that would pit him against his brother and his king?

Quinn opened his eyes and stared into the darkness. He remembered the first time he'd seen Vivian, scared and injured in the streets of Kilkerran, and he remembered thinking that they somehow had been led to that moment—that they needed each other.

He'd taken her away from that initial danger, but it was really she who had helped him on their journey this far. With her resilience and determination, she had given him hope to keep fighting for the life he truly wanted—a life he wanted to share with her. He wanted to take care of her, to see she was cherished and not used for others' gain, to love her—

Quinn started as the realization washed over him. Was he in love with Vivian? The question pierced his skull, loud and undeniable, echoing in his head, tormenting him, until the words were all he heard.

Was he in love with his brother's bride?

Quinn clenched his hands into fists. The very idea was impossible. He had never fought against his own brother before, but would he fight Reid over Vivian?

He had never wanted to fight for anything more.

Just as quickly as the thought formed, it faded. Such a battle was not his to start or even to end—it was Vivian's. Quinn, Reid, and even King James should grant her the right to choose her own future, whether that be alone as she had once told him, or beside one of them.

It was only right that she should decide her own fate.

CHAPTER FIFTEEN

THE NEXT EVENING everything happened just as Vivian's vision about Rupert's attack had foretold, except Moreis and Gillis were headed to Redhouse Castle, and Lachlan had taken Odin with him as he'd journeyed northeast toward Falkirk and the Hamilton clan.

The risk she and Quinn took was great, trying to access the cavern with Rupert on their heels, but at least by following this part of her vision it gave the others a chance to successfully bring back the help they needed to stop the Witch Hunter once and for all.

Vivian's heart thundered in her chest as her trembling fingers scraped over the cold, damp limestone. Quinn stood by her side, his sword drawn, ready to defend them if she failed to find the trigger that would open the hidden cave. "The device must be here somewhere."

"We have a lead on Rupert and his men, but not much."

Vivian heard the hoofbeats growing closer and the shouts of Rupert and his men. Her throat went dry. Speed was of the essence. Why couldn't she find the way inside? Her vision had made it all seem so easy.

Her legs turned to marble and her throat to dust as she closed her eyes and slammed her hand against the wall as she had in her vision.

Suddenly, a loud crack sounded. The mossy forest floor beneath their feet rumbled. A grinding sound vibrated in the air until a giant opening appeared in the rock face. Dirt rained down from the cliff above.

"Come on." Quinn grasped Vivian's hand and pulled her inside just as the sound of hoofbeats came from all around them. Rupert was close, but not yet in sight.

The jet-black cavern ahead terrified her, but not as much as what Rupert would do if they were captured. With her heart in her throat, Vivian stepped into the void. They had just crossed into the empty space when the sound of grinding filled the air once more.

As the wall trembled closed, the light behind them wavered, narrowed, blinked, until it vanished completely. Vivian drew a sharp breath at the finality of the sound of the stone closing. Were they trapped? Or was there a way out? Her vision had showed her nothing other than how to escape Rupert's attack.

Darkness pressed in on her, feeling unlike anything she'd experienced before. Her skin crawled. This is what being buried alive would feel like. The silence in and of itself was oppressive, suffocating.

"What do we do now?" Vivian asked. The words clung to the shadows for a long, vibrating moment, then disappeared.

"Hold tight. I saw something that might help us." Quinn dropped her hand and rustled around beside her, picking something up from the ground. Then came the sound of cloth ripping followed by a scratching noise, until a ribbon of light wavered in the void. Slowly the light intensified until it flared brightly, revealing a torch in Quinn's hands.

Vivian clasped her hands to her chest and drew a relieved breath. "Where are we?" she asked as her eyes adjusted to the light.

"This isn't a cave," Quinn said, leaving her side to light the torches that stood in readiness near the entrance. "It's an underground chamber of some sort."

Once lit, the torches created a kaleidoscope of twisting, dancing light that revealed a series of chambers hollowed out of the sandstone with high, carved archways and pillars that continued far back into the hillside.

Excitement and wonder replaced Vivian's fear and made her breath quicken. "Who would have created such a place secreted into the hillside like this?"

"Druids? Templars?" He shrugged. "This place is perfect for sheltering us from Rupert and his men for the time being."

Vivian reached out and touched the gritty sandstone walls. They were dry and cool to her touch. "Our vanishing will only make Rupert more convinced that I am a witch. At least he has no idea how we accomplished that feat."

"We are safe from Rupert for now." Quinn reached out and took her hand in his. Squeezing gently he said, "Let's make sure we are alone."

She wasn't sure what kind of inhabitants he suspected might live in this place—human or animal—but she nodded. Together, they headed through the arched passageway, moving deeper into the earthen sanctuary. The red-colored walls did not smell stale and musty like she'd expected, instead they smelled of springtime grass and sunshine. How was that possible this far inside the earth?

Carefully, they moved through the passageways. When they came to a fork, they went to the right. When they came to a dead-end that held an empty niche where a statue or relic might have once been placed, they backtracked and tried another passageway. On their third attempt they hadn't gone far when Vivian heard a soft sound. She stopped. "Mice?"

Quinn held the torch before them. "I don't think so. It sounds more like rain." As they walked, the sound intensified, then changed into that of falling water.

At first Vivian didn't believe what she was hearing, but as they continued forward the sound grew louder until they turned a corner and entered a cavernous chamber. At the back of the room foamy water tumbled downward from high overhead, splashing noisily into a naturally made pool in the rock below, sending ripples of water across the surface. Above the falling water, a halo of bluish-gray sky appeared and fresh air drifted down from above.

"A secret waterfall." Vivian stared in awe at the sight.

"It's more than that. Eventually, it's our way out of here if we cannot open the cavern door from the inside once help has arrived. It won't be an easy way out, but it'll do."

Her stomach fluttered. "Will Rupert be able to access the cavern that way?"

Quinn studied the hole in the ceiling. "I can't be certain, but I doubt he'll be looking for you at the base of a waterfall." He set down the pack he carried before opening it, removing two bedrolls and blankets along with supplies for an evening meal. "Let's set up camp for the night."

Vivian looked around the earthen cave. "There are no sticks. How will we make a fire?"

"We can't risk exposing ourselves with the smoke rising from where a waterfall disappears, so it doesn't matter that there's no fuel." He set the food sack beside her. "See what remains that we can eat cold."

She opened the satchel and found cheese, dried apples, and salted pork, which she set on a blanket she'd spread out beside the pool. If they couldn't have a fire, at least they could enjoy the view.

After setting up the rest of the camp, Quinn joined her on the blanket. She felt his gaze on her like a tangible presence. Almost a touch. Slowly she turned her head to gaze upon him fully. He was propped up on his elbows, his long legs stretched out in front of him. Their eyes met and held.

The warmth in his gaze sent a shiver skittering along her flesh. The air in the chamber seemed suddenly warmer. She swallowed and asked, "Do you think Rupert will give up searching for us in this area by morning?"

Quinn shrugged. "We will find out when we try to leave or when Malcolm signals us to come out. In the meanwhile, let us enjoy the moment. You are safe for now."

"My visions say otherwise." She couldn't hide the fear in her voice.

He sat up, suddenly tense, noticing her change in mood. "You had another vision? When?"

"Nothing more than what I've told you already."

He reached for her hand and held tight. "Have you had visions all your life?"

His touch comforted her, encouraged her to go on. "All my life I have been afraid to share what I've seen with others. Fearful of what they might do to me. Sometimes those I told accepted my gift, like Abbess Catherine. But there were others who feared me or tried to control me. King James did a little of both after I revealed my vision of an assassination attempt on his life."

Quinn's brows came together. "Obviously you foiled the attempt."

"Oh aye. After that he used my healing talents and my visions to his benefit."

"Then why did he send you away from his court and his protection?"

"Because of his growing fear that someone less under-standing would learn my secret as the hunting of witches intensified. He was concerned for my safety, whether that was for my benefit or for his own advantage, I've never been certain." She dropped her gaze to their entwined fingers and continued. "The king claimed that's why he married me to Dugald Campbell, so that I would be out of harm's way. I suppose the same considerations are why he's sending me to your brother."

"And in both instances the king has put you in further danger by exposing you to Rupert Campbell."

"I believe Dugald was to blame. The king told Dugald about my visions, and in turn I believe he told his son. 'Tis the only thing that makes sense with Rupert pursuing me as he is."

"You were betrayed by the very people who were sup-posed to protect you." Sympathy clouded Quinn's eyes, drew little lines in his forehead and tightened his mouth. "It cannot be easy for you to see things that will occur in the future. Harder still when you can share that information with only a few trustworthy people."

Vivian met his gaze. His compassion curled around her heart, bringing tears to her eyes and blurring her vision.

"Will you trust me and tell me about the vision you did not tell me about . . .the one that scared you?"

"How could you know that I did not reveal everything?"

"When you lie, you bite your lip."

"I do not," she said, biting her lip. With a sigh of resignation, she said, "In that vision I saw myself tied to a stake with flames at my feet." An uncontrollable tremble shook her. "Rupert was there, watching while I struggled to breathe and as searing pain overwhelmed me."

Quinn's features hardened. "I can understand your fear. But know this, Vivian, I will never let that happen to you. *Never.*" He clung to her hand. "I know others have promised you protection before, but I truly mean it. I have the skills and the resources to guarantee your safety, not just from Rupert, but for the rest of your life."

"With your brother's help?"

"Nay. He will protect you, of course. But if he cannot, I shall."

They would be safe once they reached Redhouse Castle. Until then, the threat to both of their lives was very real. If they were captured by Rupert before they reached the impenetrable castle walls, she would have no tomorrow and perhaps neither would Quinn. Even so, a spark of hope flickered in the darkness of her fear, illuminating the places deep inside her that she'd kept closed off for so long. Perhaps with Quinn beside her, she might find a new dream, one where she didn't have to be alone or afraid ever again.

When he brought her fingers to his lips, her heart began to pound wildly. With his eyes locked on hers, he kissed her fingertips. A heartbeat later, he turned her hand and pressed a kiss to her palm.

Vivian closed her eyes and took a deep breath as unfamiliar sensations spiraled through her body, pooling at her core. "We shouldn't . . ."

"I can't stop. I tried and I can't."

His words wound their way around her heart. "Neither can I." This moment with him transcended both time and reality—where nothing but the two of them existed and nothing else mattered.

He stood and tugged her gently to her feet. He drew her a step closer, then holding her captive with his eyes, he bent his head down and pressed his lips to her wrist.

"I want to make love to you, Vivian," he said, his voice so deep it made her shake. Vivian felt the last of her reserve fading away, melting under the dark temptation of his voice and in the fire of his heated gaze.

He drew her fully against him, allowing her hands to fall to his shoulders as his circled her waist. She wasn't trapped. Wasn't crushed. She could still pull away if she wanted to.

He lowered his head—stopped just before their lips met. He waited there so that she could sense his hunger, recognize her own.

With her next heartbeat, Vivian closed the gap. It was a relief to give in, to let all her reservations go as the yearning in her soul broke free. Longing pulsed through her, made her bold as she pressed against him, warm and willing.

He left her lips to kiss the hair at her temples, her cheek, her neck, breathing in the scent of her skin before finding her mouth once again and urging it open. As he explored her mouth, he reached up and released her hair from its plait, fanning it out over her shoulders, down her back, before he buried his fingers in its fullness while angling her head back so he could explore her mouth in deep, intimate strokes.

His arms tightened around her, crushing her breasts, already peaked and tight and aching, to the hard planes of his chest. His hand swept from her waist to the center of her back, pressing her to him, then sliding lower, over her hip, to grasp her bottom and angle her hips to his. He moved against her, molding the rigid length of his erection to her. Allowing her to anticipate having the hard length inside her. Thrusting into her, filling her, taking her to a place she'd never been before.

A shiver of desire slithered down her spine as he stripped away her gown, the pouch of herbs at her waist, her chemise, her boots and stockings until the coolness of the hidden cavern's air caressed her skin. The sensation was heightened by the heated touch of his hands, followed by the hot brand of his mouth on her throat, traveling slowly to her breast, then laying a fiery path over her stomach to ultimately taste the flesh of her thighs.

Gasping, reeling, her skin flushed, she reached for the tie of his breeches and pulled, releasing the barrier that stood between them. His other garments followed until he stood naked, bathed in the torchlight that gilded the heavy planes of his shoulders and etched the hard lines of his face. She inhaled sharply, letting her gaze slide over his muscular, battle-scared body. The injury to his shoulder was now just one of many. But even that wound had faded from an angry red to a ribbon of dull red and purple. "Does it still pain you?" she asked.

"Nay. I ache in a different way at the moment. I ache for you." He stared at her for a long moment, then ran one hand over her breast in a slow caress.

She sighed and arched into his touch, craving that sizzle of heat that slipped from his skin to hers whenever they touched. He had become as necessary to her as breathing and she wanted nothing more than to relish the feel of his hands on her body. Her heart sped up when he swept her into his arms.

"Come with me," he said, his voice tight as he carried her toward the pool.

She would have followed him anywhere. Never had she experienced such longing. She trembled as he climbed into the pool. Water splashed up on her as he moved toward the waterfall and set her on a rock ledge near the edge of the spray. Every droplet felt like a bead of fire on her skin even as the rock beneath her felt wet and slick against her bare back.

Desire uncoiled deep within her. "Please," she murmured as he took her mouth with his, not knowing what she asked for or even wanted.

After a long, exploratory kiss, his mouth left hers to slide down her jaw to her throat as he made his way to first one breast then the other, licking, nipping, and teasing as he moved back and forth until he looked up at her with hungry passion in his eyes.

Water beaded on his flesh, against her own as he moved closer between her legs. He caught her thighs and spread them apart. Naked flesh met naked flesh as his hardness probed the wetness between her legs. Her body throbbed, trembled as his shadowed gaze locked on her face. With one long, controlled thrust, he joined them.

She smothered a gasp as her hand slid down his dew-sprayed back.

He froze. His eyes flared. "You were untouched? How is that possible?"

As the pain faded and she became accustomed to his penetration, pleasure vibrated where they were joined. "Dugald never thought of me as more than his caretaker. I was his wife in name only."

Both pleasure and regret mixed in his dark eyes. "Had I known—"

"We would still be here." She arched against him.

"Aye," he acknowledged, with a renewed sparkle in his eyes. He looked at her with caring, understanding, and something more. It was the something more that made her heart swell and throat tighten. He looked at her the way a man should look at a woman. He made her feel special. Extraordinary even, and not because he saw her as a witch.

A smile touched her lips. She reached up and stroked

Quinn's cheek, felt him tremble beneath her palm. She'd gone to sleep a thousand nights dreaming about a man like him, someone who cared about her for more than what she could do for him. A man who didn't fear her gift. "Make love to me, Quinn."

A sensual smile tugged at his lips as he slowly withdrew and thrust again. His movements were agonizingly slow as the tension within her started to build, setting her nerves flickering with expectation.

She splayed her hands across his wet back, held him to her, kissed him only to be overwhelmed by the kisses he returned. She reveled in the sensation of him, so rigid, so heavy, so male, moving within her. She met him and matched him, wound her legs about his hips and drew him deeper until the sound of her heartbeat, their mingled breath, and the roar of the waterfall merged. The world around them faded until only passion and need raged like fire through her blood and into his.

He filled her, commanded her body, swamped her senses with pleasure until she was afire beneath him and something surged from deep within, wrenching all control from her.

Together they were at the mercy of whatever storm they had evoked. She cried out in surrender as pleasure exploded within her, washing through her in waves of wondrous glory.

And then she felt him stiffen, heard him cry her name as he shuddered and collapsed against her with his face buried in the curve of her neck. The heaviness of his weight felt good against her body. She could feel his heart still racing, pounding in his chest, and wished they could stay twined as they were forever, that this moment might never end.

When his breathing settled and his heartbeat slowed, Quinn rose up and looked down at her. He coiled a long strand of her now-wet hair around his finger and smiled. "That was even more perfect than I imagined it would be."

His face was so close she could see the droplets of water still clinging to his dark eyelashes. His brown eyes were tawny in the flickering light of the torches. He stared at her and she felt as if he could see straight to her soul. "Thank you for rescuing me from the villagers, for bringing me here, for caring."

"I told myself I was only doing my duty," he said as his breath brushed her cheek. "But the first time I looked into your eyes I knew that was a lie." His lips pulled up in a soft smile.

At the soft curving of his lips, Vivian felt something inside her break free. Emotion swelled with her every heartbeat. "Quinn, I . . ." The words congealed in her throat. Why couldn't she tell him how she felt in this moment? There was nothing to fear, nothing holding her back. And yet . . . Her teeth chattered.

"You're chilled. Let's get you out of the water and warm you up." He scooped her in his arms and carried her out of the water to settle her on the blanket they'd left not long ago. He sank down beside her, pulling a second blanket over them, shielding them from the chill of the night. His lips brushed her temple. "Better?"

"Aye," she replied as she nestled her head on his chest and closed her eyes. It would be so easy to give herself over to the comfortable veil of sleep. Quinn was silent beside her, his hand on her breast, his palm gentle and possessive even as exhaustion crept over them both. The moment felt like a dream, one she would hold on to forever.

QUINN'S ARMS TIGHTENED around Vivian with yearning tenderness. He shouldn't have made love to her. He shouldn't have taken what she offered, but he couldn't have stopped himself. The last few days with her at his side had shattered what had remained of his control. And now that he had taken her, he had to make things right. He had promised her protection, and he would live up to his word. If it meant moving heaven and earth to see she was safe, he would do it.

Once they escaped their current trap. And it was a trap—one he'd allowed her to lead him into. He knew better than to cut himself off, yet he would have followed her anywhere for these precious moments alone.

Quinn stared unseeing into the darkness. Stillness. The only sound in the entire cavern was that of the water falling from above. The very air around them had a timelessness about it that was both peaceful and eerie. As if the air knew that this moment he and Vivian had shared would end very soon.

Earlier, Vivian had asked if Rupert would give up his hunt for her. Quinn had managed to assuage her fears in that moment, but he knew Rupert would never give up. All tales of him said the man was clever, bold, deadly, and patient.

It was Rupert's patience that frightened Quinn the most. Even after Malcolm came to rescue them, Rupert would be out there waiting for Quinn to grow careless. Waiting for him to fall asleep when he should remain awake, to relax when he should have remained alert, to look left when he should have looked right. But that would not happen tonight.

Tonight, they were hidden from Rupert and everyone. There would be no carelessness, and, if Rupert was out there, the man would just have to wait until they emerged.

And Quinn would be ready for the Witch Hunter when they finally came face-to-face.

CHAPTER SIXTEEN

Q UINN CAME AWAKE with a start as the hairs on the back of his neck prickled. He glanced around the cavern. Only the red limestone walls stared back at him. He and Vivian couldn't be more alone, and yet he still couldn't dismiss the feeling that danger loomed just out of reach.

Vivian's foretelling of the future did not reveal all the details. Without knowing what came next, he would have to be ready for anything. If Malcolm and his men did not arrive before Rupert figured out where and how he and Vivian had disappeared, then Quinn needed an alternative plan.

He could see a ring of early morning light filtering into the cavern from the opening through which the waterfall fell. He frowned as he studied the walls around the natural formation. They were steep and smooth and they'd be as slick as ice thanks to the spray from the waterfall if they tried to climb them. Leaving the cavern that way would be difficult if not impossible without Malcolm's help from above.

Quinn disentangled himself from Vivian without waking her and sat up, gazing into the pool beside them. The water from the falls came in, yet it didn't build up, meaning the water flowed out again. If the water flowed out, then perhaps there was another way out of this place. But before they started looking into alternative ways to leave, they had to try to leave through the heavy stone wall they had entered. He should have given Lachlan a signal to use to tell them reinforcements had arrived.

Shifting his thoughts, Quinn stared down at Vivian, held captive by her beauty. Her bare skin was gilded by the sunlight streaming through from above. A riot of red hair cascaded around her shoulders and across her bare breasts. As something inside him tightened, he bent down to kiss her forehead. If this was to be their only night together for the rest of their lives, then he would be grateful for that. Until the day he died he would remember the glowing radiance on her face as they made love.

Vivian's eyes fluttered open. Her face was different this morning. Quinn smiled, seeing her eyes were alight with newfound joy.

"Is it morning already?"

"Aye," he replied, placing another kiss on her lips—a kiss she returned with infinite sweetness. When they finally broke apart, he said with regret, "Lachlan and Malcolm should be here by now. We have a better chance of success if we meet up with them before anyone else is awake."

"Rupert," she groaned and wrested the blanket aside. A heartbeat later she realized she was still naked after their lovemaking last night, and grabbed the blanket back, pulling it up to her chin.

"You cannot hide from me any longer. I familiarized my-self with every one of your charms last night." Quinn chuckled then kissed her again, quick and hard. "Come, I'll help you into your dress."

"Is that what you call them? Charms?" She gazed up at him with a smile as she lowered the blanket to reveal her breasts.

"Beautiful charms," he amended, returning her smile with a heated one of his own. If only they had more time . . .

AFTER THEY HAD both dressed and packed up camp, she and Quinn walked in silence back through the series of tunnels from which they had come. The passageway was cold and dark and disquietingly still. With only a torch to guide them, gradually Vivian's eyes became adjusted to the darkened corridors until they came to a stop before the rock face they'd entered. To the left side of the door was a large wheel that rotated on an axle and a thick rope.

"To open the door, we pull on the rope. This device will lift the heavy stone for us," Quinn said, inspecting it. "It's not unlike how a portcullis raises and lowers, except that it has a built-in system for closing itself." He pointed to the small rocks on the floor beneath a wooden bucket with a hole in the bottom. "We place these stones back in the bucket," he said as he tossed rocks inside the timing device.

"Is that why the door closed so quickly when we entered, because there were no rocks to counter-balance the weight of the door?" Vivian asked.

"Precisely."

She should have been happy at the knowledge that they were not trapped, instead she shivered, her body icy with foreboding.

"It's time to go," Quinn said after he finished adding the rocks to the bucket. He grasped the thick rope, preparing to give it a tug.

Suddenly she had a terrifying thought. "What if Rupert is on the other side?"

"He cannot know exactly where we disappeared to." Quinn paused in his motion. "But if that happens, keep him from entering while I sever the rope. The door will close as quickly as it did on us when we arrived."

"Very well." Vivian swallowed her unease and fastened her eyes on the stone doorway.

"Ready?" Quinn asked as he drew his sword with his right hand and prepared to pull the door open with his left.

With a silent prayer, Vivian nodded. Her heartbeat thrummed in her ears.

The rock wall trembled, then slowly lifted. Debris and rock rained around her, hitting the dirt floor with soft thuds. A streak of yellow light cut through the darkness, growing larger and larger until she could see outside. Sunlight splashed her face and sent warmth through her body. She took a step forward as a shape suddenly separated from the rock on her left.

"You weren't thinking of escaping me, were you?"

Vivian's stomach plummeted. Where were Lachlan and Malcolm? Their army?

Rupert came toward her with a sword in one hand and a coil of rope in the other. "Not after I've gone through so much trouble and been waiting so patiently." Malevolence echoed in his words.

Vivian took a step back. They'd been so close to freedom. Sweet Mary, she didn't want to die. She forced herself to keep her eyes trained on Rupert while Quinn busily sawed at the rope.

Rupert hadn't seen Quinn yet, which meant there was still hope of escape.

She suppressed a shiver of fear. Quinn had told her to stall Rupert if he were there, but her throat went dry and her words caught in her throat.

"Are you afraid? You're not speaking."

"Of course, I'm afraid. I'd be a fool not to be frightened of you."

"You were never a fool, but you are prey."

"You'll get no pleasure from killing me."

"You're wrong," Rupert said fiercely. "I'm going to enjoy hurting you very much."

The rope Quinn worked at snapped, the loose end whistling through the air until it snapped against the wall. In the next instant the sound of stone grinding stone echoed all around them. Dirt showered from the ceiling, scattering at her feet once more. Vivian jumped back, out of harm's way as the wall tumbled down.

"No!" Rupert's shout rose above the grinding sound until it disappeared, leaving her and Quinn in silence once more.

Vivian whirled toward Quinn as terror wormed icy tentacles through her body. The silence around them was oppressive. "Are we trapped? This time for good?"

Quinn sheathed his sword. He took her cold hand in his. "We'll leave through the waterfall."

They started the trek back to the waterfall, hand-in-hand. They were running now, the pulse in her temple pounding wildly.

"The cavern is up ahead," Quinn said, encouraging her to keep up their pace. "One more turn and we'll—"

Vivian skidded to a halt. "Nay!" Men on ropes dangled from the opening in the ceiling that the waterfall fell through. They were slowly lowering themselves inside. There were five of them, too many for her and Quinn to fight on their own.

Quinn cursed at her side. "Rupert's men."

Vivian's heart plunged. There had to be some other way out. Or should they stay and fight? "What do we do now?"

"Do you trust me?" Quinn asked.

"With my life."

"Can you swim?"

Vivian nodded. "Abbess Catherine taught me when I was young."

"Good." He ran for the pool of water, dragging Vivian behind him.

Her hip collided with the rock as he dragged her into the pool. She scarcely felt the pain as they splashed their way toward the center. Rupert's men were halfway down their ropes. In a moment or two, they would be right on top of her and Quinn. "What now?"

"The water that flows in here must leave by some means. We've got to find it and swim our way out," he said above the roar of the waterfall.

She strained to see through the green-gray water. He was right about the water not building up, but was the way that it left the cavern big enough for a person to escape through?

"Follow me," Quinn said, diving down.

Her heart hammered in her chest. If she were going to die, she would rather it be beside Quinn, struggling for their freedom, than at Rupert's hand. Drawing a deep breath, Vivian plunged below the surface.

THE JAGGED OPENING in the rock at the bottom of the pool was scarcely three feet wide. Quinn pushed his shoulders through before signaling for Vivian to follow. The rocks bit at his flesh as he swam through the dark tunnel he hoped would be their salvation.

It felt like the darkness went on forever. He could not see, but he could sense Vivian behind him as they continued on. The pressure in his chest built, tightened, squeezed, but he had no time to think of the pain. If they weren't going to make this their watery grave, they had to keep going.

His lungs ached, but he fought the near-irresistible urge to take a breath, fighting his way forward.

Then he saw it: light.

Pain seared his chest as he clawed more than swam his way through the final stretch of the tunnel. The need to breathe was all that mattered.

It was then that Quinn noticed a change. Instead of pushing against him, the water pulled him forward, faster and faster. The tunnel widened and he found himself tumbling head over foot. As he tumbled, he caught a flash of Vivian's bright red hair behind him.

Quinn tried to right himself, tried to slow himself down, to no avail. And just when he was certain his lungs would draw in that fatal pull, he felt himself thrust out of an opening and into the air.

He drew a tortured breath, only to hold it once more as he fell, cascading over a new set of falls, no more than a leaf tumbling in the churning water.

After an endless moment, he splashed into a pool and

sank into the icy depths. The plunging fall of water forced him down. Gathering all his strength, he kicked up toward the light. In a surge of effort, he broke through the surface and hitched in a convulsive breath, taking in near as much water as air. As he choked and coughed, Vivian's body emerged beside him.

Quinn grasped her by the arm and hauled her against his chest. Fear lodged in his throat. Her body was limp. Feeling the flesh of her exposed throat, he sought a beat.

Then he felt it: the gentle pulse of her life's blood against his finger. He drew a ragged breath as he searched her face.

Her eyes were closed and her skin had turned a purplish blue. "Vivian! For God's sake, breathe." He shook her hard. "Breathe! Breathe!"

She went rigid. Her eyes cracked open. She dragged in a shallow breath, then a deeper one, which caused her to sputter and cough up the water she had inhaled.

Her skin flushed pink and her eyes flickered open, focusing on him.

"We made it," he said.

Her response was a groan as he carried her out of the water then set her on the shore. He pulled her into his arms and held her folded body. "It's going to be all right," he crooned over and over again as her strength slowly returned.

Finally, she looked at him. Her eyes filled with defeat. "Will we ever escape Rupert?"

"We already have. As long as we are together, nothing

can tear us apart."

Her eyes glistened as she fought back tears. "Together."

Invisible hands clutched his heart and squeezed. *I'm sorry, Reid.* Quinn tightened his hold on the woman in his arms. He could never give her up to his brother. He would accept whatever punishment he had to—even banishment—but he would never let Vivian go.

"Has your strength returned enough to stand?" he asked.

"I think so," Vivian replied.

"We have to keep moving if we are to stay ahead of those who hunt us." Rupert's men could follow them through the tunnel at any moment. Quinn helped Vivian up and made certain she was steady on her feet before he released her. He looked left and right, trying to see if Lachlan and Malcolm had finally arrived. Seeing nothing, he tried to get his bearings.

The waterfall had dumped them out of the hillside below a group of impressive crags. It was an area he recognized as the Gargunnock Hills located to the west of Stirling. "We need to head east. Are you—"

Something cracked into the back of his head with a sickening thud. Pain exploded behind his eyes. He wobbled and fell to his knees against the hard rock. He clutched the hilt of his sword and tried to draw it free as he struggled to focus his gaze on the area nearest them.

He could see no one, but he knew Rupert was there.

He had to protect Vivian.

Slick, warm blood oozed down Quinn's neck as he clung on to consciousness. With an agonized groan he collapsed on the rock ledge, still searching for whoever had attacked him.

He had to keep Vivian safe.

"Quinn?"

Vivian's voice echoed in his ears. Everything slowed to a crawl. His vision narrowed to a pinpoint. Through a distant, fuzzy part of his brain he heard the shuffle of feet, heard Vivian scream.

Rupert had found them.

Vivian! Fury clashed with his fading senses. He'd promised her he would keep her safe. Quinn struggled to stay conscious. Clawing at the rock beneath him with his fingertips, he pulled himself toward the sound of her voice.

He could feel the world around him slipping away. Fear rose up fast and sank inside him. He felt heavy, leaden.

And then the world went dark.

CHAPTER SEVENTEEN

P ANIC AND HORROR seized Vivian as Quinn collapsed in a heap. She scrambled to his side as blood oozed from a wound to the back of his head. Beside him, a red-stained rock glistened in the spray from the waterfall. Quinn's eyes were closed, and his face was so pale it looked nearly blue.

The sound of footsteps echoed all around her. She looked up to the ridge. Rupert stood there, flanked by two of his men.

They had to get out of there and fast. "Quinn?" Urgently, Vivian shook his shoulder.

No response.

Her heart hammering in her chest, she ripped a length of cloth from her chemise and tied it around Quinn's head before standing and trying to lift him. His dead weight pulled at her arms. He was too heavy.

In the next instant, a pair of arms grasped her shoulders and jerked her backward against a man's chest.

She tried to wrench away, but he was too strong. "There is no escape for you, little witch."

Vivian spun around to stand face-to-face with Rupert.

His hair was wet and slicked back from his forehead, making him look even more sinister than usual. His cold, merciless fingers curled around her arm, squeezing tight.

Despite all their efforts to escape, Rupert had found them after all. Vivian started to shake. Desperately, she tried to hide her fear, clenching her fists at her sides and biting her lip. She had to stay in control, to clamp the panic down, to keep it from showing. She wouldn't give Rupert any more power over her than he already had.

"Let's go. I have plans for you." Rupert dragged her away from Quinn, heading up a trail to the left of the waterfall. The path was steep and traversed back and forth.

"Quinn needs help." Vivian dug her heels into the hillside.

"If he's smart he'll stay where he is." Rupert jerked her off her feet, propelling her forward.

More scared than she'd ever been in her life, Vivian regained her balance and kicked out wildly in a blind attempt to free herself. She connected with Rupert's groin.

He grunted in pain and released his hold on her arm.

In that split second of his surprise, she pulled away, racing down the hillside without a backward glance.

"Quinn!" she cried out, hoping he would regain consciousness and help her fight. If not, perhaps she could roll him into the water and the two of them could float away.

Or be easily drowned when Rupert caught up with her.

Vivian forced the ugly thought away. Panting, she

slipped and slid down the moist ground, fighting to keep herself from falling as she made her way back to Quinn's side.

Please, God, she prayed. *Help us!*

Even before her prayer was fully formed, she heard Rupert thrashing through the vegetation behind her. She surged forward in the same instant that she was jerked back into the wall of Rupert's chest. The deadly edge of a knife pressed against her throat. "You stupid witch! You'll pay for that, I promise!" he snarled.

Vivian's heart fell. The knife's edge bit into her skin. She could feel Rupert's hot, moist breath on her cheek.

Not ready to give up yet, Vivian jabbed her elbow into his gut.

Rupert grunted.

The pressure of the knife lessened, yet when she twisted, she felt the blade catch her flesh. A warm trickle of blood ran down her throat. It didn't matter. She balled her fists and slammed them into Rupert's chest, right in the center of his breastbone.

His eyes flared wide as he choked and staggered backward. The knife fell from his hands.

She scooped up the knife. Her mind raced and her heart beat frantically in her chest as she hurried back to Quinn. Before she could reach his prone body, she froze.

Three men with their hair and clothing dripping stood beside Quinn, their swords drawn. He was still unconscious, but the mercenaries had bound him at the hands and the legs.

Vivian held the knife before her, taking a defensive stance, even though she knew she was no match for their strength or their swords.

In the next heartbeat, Rupert was behind her. He grabbed her waist, holding her so tight she could scarcely breathe. He plucked the knife from her hand. "Meet my men," Rupert growled against her ear as the knife pressed against her throat once more. She could feel the warmth of her own blood trailing down her throat. "Stop fighting me. It's over for both you and your protector."

Rupert tightened his hold on her waist and dragged her toward his men. Their features were taut and they wouldn't meet her gaze. They feared her, she realized, as two men grabbed her feet while the other tied them together before moving on to her hands. When they were done, they flinched away as though afraid of what she might do to them, even bound. She could not hurt them—but they didn't know that.

Rupert removed his knife and shoved her to the ground beside Quinn. "All right, Witch. Time to pay for your sins."

Vivian drew in deep, terrified breaths as her heartbeat thundered in her ears. "You're wrong about me. I'm not a witch."

"That's what your kind always say." Rupert laughed. "But I know the truth. My father told me all about how you cast a spell on him. How you drained the life from him. How you killed him in the end."

Lies.

The taste of fear was sharp and bitter on her tongue. She shivered, and avoided meeting the men's gazes, trying to keep her features from betraying her thoughts. She was out of time and out of hope. Quinn was the only person who could have come to her rescue, and not even he could keep her safe from Rupert and his lies any longer.

Rupert turned to Vivian; his eyes were bright with excitement. "I was going to kill Quinn here, making his death seem like a tragic accident so as not to bring retribution to me from his brother and the Douglas clan; however, your unwillingness to leave him has given me a different idea."

"What is that?" Vivian asked. "You realize the risk you take in harming either of us, accidentally or otherwise? Quinn is one of the king's special guards. I am his ward. If anything happens to us, King James and Reid Douglas will hunt you down."

Rupert laughed. "I can do what I want to whom I want. By the authority of the king, I can capture and question anyone I suspect of using witchcraft." Rupert's features hardened. "And I suspect you both." He shook her until her teeth rattled in her head. "Now prepare yourself. We'll ride hard the rest of the day and through the night."

Vivian swallowed roughly. "Where are you taking us?"

"To the witches' tribunal in North Berwick."

Vivian went still in Rupert's arms. "I will go willingly if you leave Quinn here. I'll do whatever you want, say whatever you want me to say. Leave him out of all this."

Rupert's eyes narrowed. "I won't fall for your tricks. You'll say what I want you to say because you'll have no choice as I force you to watch while I slowly and painfully drain the life from Quinn Douglas's body."

Vivian could not hold back a shudder of fear. This wasn't part of her vision but that didn't mean it wouldn't happen. There would be no help for her or Quinn on the journey to North Berwick. She could try to scream, to draw attention to herself and to Quinn, but no one would come to their aid. The people of Scotland no longer cared what happened to a witch or a cunning man as long as they did not live or practice the dark arts in their village.

Vivian still couldn't understand how all this was happening. Most of those who were captured had been women, and it was impossible to believe they'd been aught but ordinary humans, with no powers at all. Rupert and others locked them away, put them on trial, and executed them, giving them little hope of any other outcome.

"Don't let your guard down," the Witch Hunter cautioned his men as they carried Quinn up the path by his feet and shoulders. Rupert escorted her up the path behind them. His gaze met hers. She tried not to cringe from the hatred reflected in his dark eyes. "There's no telling what a trapped witch will do. You're all evil down to the core. And I for one will not rest until you're all burned at the stake."

Fear clawed at her chest as she looked into Rupert's eyes. She saw her own death written there.

A DULL THUD pounded through Quinn's head. Each throbbing beat brought a stab of pain spiking through his skull. He swallowed past the dryness of his throat, tasting something metallic.

They had been attacked.

Full consciousness hit Quinn like a blow, and his eyes snapped open.

Vivian. Rupert had captured Vivian.

Terror, colder than anything he'd experienced before stole his breath. He became chillingly aware of the semidarkness surrounding him, the odor of the damp earth, the smell of pitch and decay. Light from a window slit filtered into the small chamber around him. He was lying in a dungeon, nestled amongst some rotting hay.

Where was Vivian?

Quinn looked around the chamber. He was alone.

Needing to get his bearings, he sat up. At the sudden movement, his head spun. Nausea roiled in the pit of his stomach. He waited for his stomach to ease before he stretched out his legs only to realize he was chained to the floor by two iron manacles wrapped around his ankles. The rattling of the chains echoed in the emptiness of the room.

Slowly he stood, keeping the nausea at bay until he stretched toward the window slit. A wisp of fresh air came to Quinn and he drew a deep breath, easing the tightness in his lungs. A heartbeat later, that breath arrested and a shiver went down his spine at the sight of a young woman in a cloak being dragged toward a platform where a crowd gathered around. They were at some sort of tribunal.

The cold settled deeper, pinching Quinn's lungs until the young woman reached the dais and one of the men yanked the cloak from her shoulders revealing a head of blonde hair.

Not Vivian. Relief rushed through Quinn as the woman in shackles was brought to stand before a man he recognized as King James. A scowl of displeasure marred the king's face as he took in her torn and soiled clothing and the wild tangle of her hair. The king accepted a piece of parchment from the Lord Advocate beside him and read, "Euphemia Maclean, you have been named as a witch by Agnes Sampson who recently delivered your child. She claims you accepted a potion during your delivery to cut your pain, and in doing so you sought to obtain supernatural powers by making a pact with Satan."

The king looked up, addressing the woman. "Are you ready to tell us what promises Satan made you?"

"I've never had contact with the Devil."

"Did you believe Satan's lies?"

Her response was a choked sob.

"If you will not answer the questions, then you leave me no choice but to search for a witch's mark. That will tell whether you are an agent of Satan or not." With the rise of his hand, he set the examination in motion. "Search for a mark."

The crowd cheered as the young woman's clothes were stripped from her body.

"Burn the witch!"

"She's an ally of Satan."

"String her up!"

"Magic is evil."

Quinn watched in horror as the young woman's bare skin was examined from her head to her toes for anything that could be construed as a mark given to her by Satan. Her belly was wrinkled and slightly distended. Her breasts were swollen and red from her recent pregnancy. Had she still been with child she might have been spared. But since she'd already given birth the examination would continue.

The guards poked and prodded the young woman, whose face had gone from pale to ghostly white. She staggered on the platform, appearing as though she barely had the strength to hold herself upright while the humiliating search continued. When the guards found nothing upon her exposed flesh, they lifted her arms to take their probe to a more intimate level.

"She has a scar beneath her right arm," one of the guards called out over the jeers of the crowd.

"I fell out of a tree when I was eight years old and cut myself on a stick," the accused tried to explain.

"Is it a devil's mark?"

"Only one way to find out," the Lord Advocate said solemnly.

The taller of the two guards stepped forward and accepted a pin from the Lord Advocate. The instrument of torture was thin and long. The myth was that if the woman had truly denounced her baptism, and if this were a mark, then the scar would not bleed.

As the guard drove the pin into her scar, the young woman cried out in agony.

When no blood came forth, the crowd cheered. "She's a witch! Take her to Castlehill and burn her!"

Quinn clenched his jaw so hard he was surprised the bones didn't crack. *God's bones! Would they do the same to Vivian?*

Quinn eased away from the window slit to stand in the semi-darkness once more. He clutched his hands at his sides as fury and horror rumbled through him. He wanted to strike something. Badly. If he were free from this prison, and if he had a sword . . .

He had to find a way to escape this prison. He had to find Vivian. To protect her. Ignoring the pull of the heavy shackles against his skin, he stretched toward the door. "Guard! I need to see a guard!" After what seemed like an eternity, the door of his cell squeaked open. "Good. You're awake." Rupert Campbell stepped into the cell with a torch in hand. "I was worried we had done you some grievous physical damage when you didn't wake right away. You've been senseless for the better part of two days." He held the torch out, revealing his ruddy face and bright eyes as he tried to force Quinn back.

Quinn remained where he was, unyielding. *Two days?* What had they done to Vivian in that time? Temper and desperation welled up inside him as he lurched against his restraints. He drew a tight breath, forcing his rage aside. He had to remain calm. He had to think clearly. When his breathing settled, he asked, "Where is Vivian?"

Rupert shifted to the side, keeping the flame between them. "So worried about the witch when you should be worried about yourself."

"Tell me, where is she?"

"She's alive for now." Rupert's voice lowered to silken softness.

Quinn thrilled at the knowledge but did not relax. This wasn't over yet. "I demand to see King James."

Rupert inclined his head in a mocking bow. "You demand? Have you forgotten who is the prisoner here?"

"As a member of the king's elite guard I have every right to make such a demand, and the king will come down upon you for not honoring my request."

Rupert's gaze narrowed on Quinn's face. "You have no rights. You've been accused of witchcraft."

Quinn straightened. "By whom?"

"Me."

"I've done nothing that can be interpreted as sorcery."

"Haven't you?" A smug grin etched across Rupert's face. "I recall watching you lift then lower a wall of rock."

"Through the use of a gear system similar to that used to raise and lower a portcullis. You and I have both seen how a castle gate works many times."

"That was not what I saw." Rupert's grin faded. "You used magic to close yourself off from me and avoid capture."

"My word against yours."

Rupert's features turned to stone. "My opinion is all that matters."

"Are you willing to put your lies on trial? The truth will come out during questioning—questioning that is conducted by King James, I've been told."

"The king does question those accused, but I intend to have a full confession from you long before you step in front of the man."

"With torture."

Rupert's smile returned. "It works every time."

"Until now. Prepare to be disappointed."

Rupert flinched. "We'll see about that." He moved to the doorway and yelled to the guards, "Take him to the rack."

A blast of cold, mold-laden air washed over Quinn. He steeled himself against what was to come by allowing a carefully tempered rage to rise from within him. Torture he could endure. Losing Vivian, he could not.

CHAPTER EIGHTEEN

"TELL ME, WHAT knowledge do you have of—" A commotion at the door caused King James to lose his concentration. He'd had the perfect question in mind to ask the accused witch before him. The question would have determined once and for all whether the woman should be prosecuted or not.

Frustration rose in James as he turned toward the disturbance to see a small woman with stark-white hair arguing with the guards.

"I must see the king. 'Tis urgent that I do," she yelled from the doorway, causing a stir amongst the gathered crowd.

Two guards grabbed the older woman by the arms, hauling her backward out of the door. The woman's thin, sallow face flushed in distress. "Yer Grace, Vivian, Lady Campbell, is in trouble."

The name and the urgency in the old woman's voice sent a ripple of fear down the king's spine. He stood. "Bring the woman to me," James commanded.

The woman was led forward, her arms still locked at her

sides by his overprotective guards. She bowed her head. "Thank ye, Yer Grace. 'Twas most urgent I see ye."

"Release her," James said to the guards. They dropped their hold on the woman but remained nearby, and for that James was grateful. There'd been too many attempts on his life as of late. Assassins could take any number of forms . . . that of an old woman or even a witch. He had to be careful. "What did you say about Vivian?"

"Ye must help her."

James's brows came together. He had helped his ward more than he had most others in his care. What could she need now? "You're giving me orders?"

The woman dropped to her knees before him. "Yer Grace, I meant nae offense. 'Tis an urgent situation."

James looked about the chamber. All eyes were on him. This would never do. In order to protect his ward and himself, he had to keep all information regarding her private. With a raise of his hand, he dismissed the chamber. When the guards hesitated, he said, "You as well, though stay by the door should I have need of you."

When he and the older woman were finally alone, he said, "Go on."

"I was Vivian's maid and protector while she was married to Dugald Campbell."

"The woman Abbess Catherine recommended. Gillis Drummond."

The older woman nodded. "I stayed with Vivian through

the months of her marriage, and through her husband's death."

James frowned. "Unfortunate that Dugald Campbell didn't last as long as I'd hoped he might."

"Aye, and so, my liege, the girl's in trouble. Her marriage exposed her tae Dugald's son. He's a dangerous man."

"That is why I betrothed her to Reid Douglas. To protect her once again." James's frown increased. "If she has safely arrived in his care, then why do you ask for my intervention?"

"She never arrived. She was captured."

"By whom?" James asked.

"By Rupert Campbell. He has brought her here, tae the tribunal, and has publicly accused her of being a witch."

"What do you mean, she's here?" James bent forward and grasped the woman's arm. "She was supposed to be protected."

"Quinn Douglas tried tae protect her, but Rupert is as wicked as they come."

James's eyes flared. "Quinn? What happened to Reid?"

"She would have been nae safer with Reid Douglas, ye know that."

He did know that, James acknowledged. The Douglas twins were both fearsome warriors. Two of his best men. But Rupert Campbell was also very good at his job. He'd rounded up more witches in the last month than they had all of last year. The man had earned the name the Witch Hunter of Scotland because he was very good at his job.

"Ye must free her," Gillis pleaded. "Only ye can."

"If she has been publicly charged by Rupert, then not even I can stop what has been set in motion until she goes to trial." James's voice trembled with both fear and rage. How could all his plans to keep her safe have failed? "How long has she been here?" James asked, trying to sort out this travesty in his mind.

"She arrived this mornin' with Quinn Douglas."

He narrowed his gaze on her face. "How is it that you know all this?"

"Vivian tried tae send me away after she had a vision— my liege, ye know of her visions."

At his acknowledgment, Gillis went on. "She had a vision that those of us travelin' with her would be captured and possibly killed if we stayed together. So we split up. But instead of goin' where I was directed, I followed m'lady. That's when I saw Rupert capture Vivian and Quinn and bring 'em here." The older woman's eyes were wild in her pale face. "Stop the rest of her vision from comin' true. Please, don't let Rupert kill her."

Frustration, acid hot and bile bitter, tore through James. How had it come to this point? With Vivian here at the tribunal, there was little more he could publicly do. If Vivian was proven a witch, then she would have to suffer the consequences like all the others who had come before her.

Or would she?

He was still the king. These were his trials. James went still. There was one way . . . "I have an idea, or should I say there is someone who can help us. I need to send for her. It should not take long."

Gillis nodded even as tears formed in her eyes. "That's more than I ever hoped fer, Yer Grace." She bowed and backed away to a respectful distance. "May I beg ye one more favor?"

What more could she want? He paused, glaring at the older woman.

Gillis averted her gaze. "May I see her, even if 'tis only fer a moment?"

The king's tension eased. "Aye. I'll have one of the guards escort you to her. While you are there, please tell Vivian I am working on her behalf. That knowledge might give her hope."

"YOU'LL GET . . . nothing . . . from me." Quinn choked out the words. The sound was almost a sob but he reined it in before it could betray him. His arms and legs were pulled taut, then stretched even further with a crank of the wheel on the torturous device. He could feel his muscles quivering, too near to ripping at the brutal assault.

Rupert's face went red with fury. "What do I have to do to break you? I've already dislocated both of your shoulders.

One more crank of the wheel and I'm certain your arms will snap off."

Sweat beaded on Quinn's forehead and streaked down his cheeks, pooling in his ears and along the base of his neck. Exhausted by all he'd endured, he lay biting his lower lip to hold back a scream of agony.

He was dying. Rupert was killing him.

Hatred boiled acid black inside him. It was better to let the anger fester than give in to the fear.

He *wouldn't* die.

He'd live.

Because he couldn't die while Rupert Campbell would hurt Vivian.

The door of the chamber crashed against the wall, the noise echoing through the small chamber. "What in God's name is happening here?"

Quinn released an agonized breath at the sound of King James's voice.

Rupert's hand left the crank, releasing the tension.

A shiver of relief ran through Quinn at the reprieve.

Rupert's body went rigid as he turned to offer the king a bow. "This man is charged with being an accomplice to witchcraft and helping a daughter of Satan escape capture." Rupert straightened.

"He's done no such thing." James came to stand beside the rack, his eyes gleaming brilliantly despite the semi-darkness of the torture chamber.

"I am sorry for all of this," said the king, gently touching Quinn's abused shoulder. "Release him at once." James's hand fell away.

"Your Grace, I must object. This man is a danger—"

"You will do as I command," James said, straightening to his full height. "I gave you license to hunt down witches, not my own men."

"This man is—"

"This man is no slave of the devil. He is a warrior, and one of my best. I need him and the contingent he commands in order to protect my kingdom." King James's lips tightened until they formed a thin line. "If you cannot abide by that, then I have no need of you."

Rupert glared at the king. "And you can find witches on your own, can you?"

Unfazed by Rupert's anger, the king turned back to the door and signaled for someone to enter. "As a matter of fact, I have a new helper in my quest to purge this country of evil. Laird Campbell meet Mrs. Aitken."

The tall, thin woman came forward and bowed before the king. He waved her up, motioning toward the rack. "Mrs. Aitken has a special ability. She can look in a person's eyes and tell if they are a witch or not."

"It can't be true," Rupert scowled.

A smug smile came to the king's face. "She's quite adept at seeing a secret mark in a witch or a cunning man's eyes." He paused to address the woman. "Mrs. Aitken, please tell me what you see in this man's eyes."

Quinn held his breath.

The woman leaned over him and peered into his face. Her expression remained blank as she straightened. "He bears no mark. This man is innocent."

Relief poured through Quinn in a dizzying stream.

"Release him, Campbell, before I have Mrs. Aitken look in your eyes." Triumph brought a tinge of pink to the king's cheeks.

Rupert's face darkened as he removed his dagger from its sheath on his belt and slit the ropes at Quinn's hands and feet.

Quinn struggled to sit up. Every muscle in his body spasmed taut. Pain screamed from his shoulders all the way down to his toes. The harsh, ragged tenor of his breathing scored the silence that had fallen over the room. Ignoring it all, he stood, and sank to the floor in a dead faint.

Chapter Nineteen

VIVIAN STUMBLED AS the guards shoved her into a small cell and slammed the door shut. All around her echoed the screams and cries of others who were believed to be witches. She knew what happened in places like this. How men and women were tortured until they confessed to any crime just to make the punishment stop.

It didn't matter if any of them were innocent or guilty, not when it was assumed that witches and cunning men were to blame for all the misfortune that had fallen over Scotland in the past several years.

It didn't matter that she was innocent.

Rupert would see she suffered as much if not more than the others. And in the end, he would drag her to a stake all because she was different than those around her.

Not special.

Just different.

And because she had crossed his path.

"God help me," she prayed into the musty air, hoping for a miracle.

A shiver racked her. She wrapped her arms around herself in a vain attempt to ward off a chill. The walls were damp and cold, the air stale and pungent. Shadows flickered eerily from the torches set into iron sconces on the walls in the corridor.

Vivian stood rigid in the corner of her cell, too afraid to sit or lie down as she heard mice scurrying in the darkened corners. The chill seeped into her bones as the hours passed, until a new sound separated from the others—footsteps coming her way.

She tensed, every muscle becoming rigid as the sound came closer. After handing her over to the guards, Rupert had threatened to return to question her. He'd looked at her with cool, unfeeling eyes as he'd stroked her bruised cheek and whispered of the pain to come.

She would endure whatever agony she had to if it kept Rupert away from Quinn. Vivian wasn't sure if she was more grateful that Quinn had remained unconscious during their journey to Haddington or terrified that Rupert might have done him irreparable harm. If only she knew what had happened to Quinn since they'd arrived, she might breathe a little easier.

The footsteps grew closer.

Vivian felt a flash of fear but quickly conquered it. She wouldn't be able to endure what came next, what her vision had shown her, if she were afraid.

The footsteps stopped and the door swung open. It wasn't Rupert, but a familiar female silhouette outlined against the flickering amber glow of the torch lighting the corridor. A moment later the door closed behind her. "Gillis? How are you here?" Vivian's knees went weak.

Gillis came forward to steady her. "My sweet girl. What have they done tae ye?"

A spark of hope flickered in the darkness of Vivian's fear. "Are you here to take me away?" She was afraid to move or even breathe.

Gillis's eyes filled with tears as she shook her head. "If that were possible, I'd take ye from here and never look back." Tears rolled down her cheeks. "The king allowed me tae see ye. I had tae make certain ye were well."

Gillis's gaze passed from the bruise on her cheek to the tear in her bodice, to the scrap on her neck, and finally to the deep cut on the back of her hand. Rupert had delivered them all as a reminder to her that he was in control of her future.

"It will take more than a few scrapes and bruises to break me," Vivian said, forcing bravery into her words, but she could not stop the trembling that set into her limbs.

Gillis wrapped her arms tightly around Vivian, pulling her close. "My dear, sweet, brave, wonderful girl."

Vivian's breath caught at the unexpected show of affection. Warmth seeped from Gillis's body into hers, reminding Vivian that she was not alone—that she wouldn't be alone, even at the end.

Vivian burrowed closer until the trembling in her limbs stopped and she felt at peace once more. After a long while, she eased back and smiled at her friend. "I'm not afraid anymore."

Lines of weariness and sorrow showed on Gillis's face. "The king asked me to tell you that he is working on your behalf."

Vivian shook her head in confusion. "He told me long ago if I were captured he could do nothing to help."

"Nay, you're wrong. So many of us are working tae help ye. I do nae know what happened to Lachlan and Malcolm, but Moreis and Reid Douglas should arrive with reinforcements soon. Until they do, ye must trust that the king, myself, and Quinn will do everythin' we can."

Quinn. "Have you seen him? Is he all right?"

"I've nae seen Quinn since yer arrival at the tolbooth. But in my heart, I know he's well, and that he'll come fer ye."

The passionate force of Gillis's words caused a faint stirring of hope to blossom inside Vivian.

"How is it that you are here when Moreis and Lachlan are not?"

Gillis's gaze dropped to her feet. "I disobeyed ye when ye told me tae go with Moreis. Instead, I followed ye and Quinn. If only I could have stopped Rupert from—"

"That's all in the past." Vivian stopped her from saying anything more. "I am very glad to see you once again before I die."

"Ye won't die!" Gillis's eyes filled with moist brilliance.

Vivian forced a soft smile. "All right. If I die."

If.

A world of hope weighted that one single word. *If* meant there was a possibility of a future for her, for Quinn, for the two of them together. And *if* they were thinking of the future, then she needed help from the woman before her. "Gillis, I need to ask two things of you."

"Anything." Gillis's voice was thick.

Vivian started to unlace her skirt. "First, take off your skirt and trade it with mine. I'll not have everything I've saved go to anyone but you *if* the worst should happen."

Gillis knew she talked about the cairngorm, garnet, sapphires, and amethyst gemstones she had concealed in the hem of her gown. With a quick nod, Gillis took off her skirt and swapped it with Vivian's.

"Secondly, I need you to find out *if* Quinn is . . ."

"I'll find him, love. Don't ye worry. I'll find him and send word tae ye. Though from what I saw while the two of ye were alone together, it'll take more than Rupert Campbell or an injury tae his head tae keep Quinn away from ye."

"Thank you." The knot in Vivian's throat made it hard to say more. Gillis knew as well as Vivian that her chances of leaving the tribunal alive were slim. But she wouldn't spend her final days or hours in fear. Not anymore. She was ready to grasp the possibility of a rescue with every part of her being.

A rap came on the door a moment before it opened.

"Time's up. Let's go," said a burly guard who stuck his head inside the darkened chamber.

After a quick goodbye, Gillis left. Before the door fully closed, it creaked open again. This time Rupert stood there with a lantern in one hand and rope in the other. "I've come to hear your confession." His voice resonated in the chamber and in her soul.

Vivian steeled herself. "You'll get no confession from me."

Hatred glittered in his gaze. "You're wrong. I always get your kind to confess." He held out the coil of rope to her. "Form a loop and slip it around your wrists."

Vivian didn't move.

"Either you put the rope around your wrists or I call the guards to do it for you. If I end up calling the guards, they will expect that we proceed with your questioning as we usually do by stripping you down and parading you out in front of a crowd to search for a witch's mark."

His icy gaze connected with hers. "You choose: a private interrogation or a public humiliation."

She had little choice. Vivian took the rope, formed a noose, and slipped it around her wrists.

"Good." Rupert tightened the rope then gave it a jerk, testing it. "That should hold you for the time being." He set the lantern down before grasping the end of the rope like a lead. "It's time for you to pay for bewitching my father."

Her stomach pitched. "Is that what you would have everyone believe? I did nothing of the sort. Anyone at Kilkerran can tell you I cared for him and eased his pain with no witchcraft at all."

"Many of the residents of Kilkerran have sworn to me that the opposite is true. That you are a witch. That you did use witchcraft to send my father to his death."

"Nay."

Rupert's hand cracked against her cheek with such force she fell to the ground.

Vivian shook her head, trying to clear it of the ringing pain of Rupert's blow.

"You must not lie to me." Rupert frowned down at her in the lamplight. "Then there is the matter of your visions."

Vivian went cold. He would have difficulty forming a case against her with regard to her care of Dugald Campbell. Proving she had visions would be difficult, but not impossible if Quinn or Gillis or any of the sisters at Inishail were tortured into betraying her.

Had he tortured Quinn already? As quickly as the thought formed she dismissed it. If Rupert had a confession of her guilt, then he wouldn't be standing before her, trying to extract that same information from her. The thought brought a measure of comfort.

Rupert bent down and effortlessly lifted Vivian to her feet. He stared down at her, drinking in her pain. "You could save us both a lot of trouble and simply confess. Or I can put you through the same horrors that another of your kind was subjected to this morning."

Perverse pleasure flitted through his dark eyes. "The witch used dark magic to alleviate pain. I'm a believer that a witch's punishment should fit her crime. Do you know what I did to her?"

Vivian's throat went dry.

"After I stripped her naked, I tied her to the stake atop a pyre and drove stakes through her arms, and legs, and chest." He smiled wickedly. "The poor thing suffered agonizing pain, far worse than that of childbirth, before I burned her alive. Her screams lasted for ten full minutes. A fitting death, don't you think?"

He was a monster. Vivian could imagine all too well the agony the poor girl must have experienced at Rupert's hands.

He came closer. "Does that frighten you, Vivian?"

He wanted her fear. She could see it in his expression. She didn't answer.

"Are you ready to tell me the truth? Are you a witch?"

Vivian knew she was grasping at her last straw but she said the one thing she could think of that might help her. She flicked her eyes open. "I want to see King James."

Rage colored Rupert's face. "It was a vision, wasn't it? That's how you knew to send the king to keep me from making Douglas talk?"

"Quinn's awake? Alive?" The words tumbled out. She regretted them the moment they took form.

Rupert's expression slid into pleasure. "He's dead. I

pulled his arms clean off and he bled to death before my very eyes."

Pain tore through Vivian, piercing her to the depths of her soul. Her world shifted and her heart shattered in waves of agony. She couldn't breathe. The fear she'd tried to keep at bay closed in on her. Quinn couldn't be dead. She would know if he was. She would feel something . . . Her body started to shake as anguish took hold.

A jerk on the rope brought her back to the here and now. "Are you ready to confess?" Rupert demanded.

Nausea roiled in her stomach. She was so afraid. But she wouldn't let him know it. Clutching her hands at her sides, she tried to be strong. "Why do you need my confession? You'll kill me no matter what I say."

"True," he admitted. "Will you tell me what I want to hear?"

"That time passed when you failed to leave Quinn behind." She struggled against the restraints.

Satisfaction gleamed in his eyes.

She'd given him exactly what he wanted.

"Then you leave me no choice." With a smile, he jerked her toward the door.

She dug in her heels, resisting. Her efforts were in vain as he dragged her into the corridor and down the empty hall. Her heartbeat thundered in her ears and the taste of fear was bitter on her tongue. She squirmed against the restraints. If she could slow him down someone might see them and step in to help her. "Stop, please . . . If you won't take me to the king, then I demand to see the Lord Advocate."

Rupert stopped. "You demand? You have no rights, Witch. I decide who you see and when. Now shut up." His tone was fierce. He thrust his hand into his tunic and came out with a length of cloth. "As a matter of fact, I think I'll silence you for good."

"Nay!" She drew a deep, terrified breath as he reached up and fixed the gag to her mouth. She was out of time and out of hope. No one was coming to her rescue, not this time. And the one person who might have cared enough to save her was dead.

Rupert would burn her at the stake.

Her vision was becoming reality, a horrible, hideous reality, from which there was no escape.

CHAPTER TWENTY

WHEN QUINN NEXT opened his eyes, it was to see King James sitting beside him on a bed. The man's image swam in and out of focus. They'd given him something to lessen the pain. A dull throbbing hovered just out of reach, for which he was grateful.

"I was hoping you wouldn't wake yet," King James said with a grimace. "The court physician is here. He's going to put your shoulders back in place."

Quinn stiffened, his gaze flying across the room. A tall, thin man dressed in a blue tunic advanced toward the bed. "No doubt I will regret waking in a moment. I have no fondness for pain."

"We gave you laudanum, but that's not likely to be enough." King James's lips thinned. "You have suffered terribly at Rupert Campbell's hands. I blame myself for that. I knew his methods for hunting witches and extracting confessions was somewhat unconventional, but I had no idea to what extent he pushed his authority. I'm sorry you were caught up in all that."

"It matters not. I am alive. With your permission, I shall

deal with Rupert Campbell once I am able."

"Not until you are able," King James replied, consenting to Quinn's request.

"Then let us make that happen as quickly as possible so the man harms no one else." Quinn's gaze shifted from the king to the physician.

"Good afternoon, sir," the man said with good humor. "I'm Dr. Parkins. I'll soon have your shoulders back where they belong."

What had Vivian implored him to do while she mended his shoulder? *Think of something beautiful.* Quinn smiled at the memory and fixed an image of her in his mind's eyes. "I'm ready."

The doctor nodded and ran his hands along Quinn's right shoulder. "Brace yourself—" The man pulled hard and rotated Quinn's arm.

Vivian's image faltered. Searing, white-hot pain ripped through Quinn. A pop sounded and his shoulder slid back into the socket.

"Very good," the doctor said cheerfully, switching his position to the other side of the bed. The doctor's hands moved to Quinn's left shoulder, grasping his arm firmly.

Quinn tried to focus on Vivian once again, but before he could, pain erupted and rippled through his entire body. His back arched off the bed as the joint slipped back into place. He lay panting, the room whirling around him.

"That does it. You're as good as new." The physician

turned away from the bed. "I would recommend you stay abed for at least a week and let your body heal."

"Impossible," Quinn said as he tried to sit. "I must get to Vivian before Rupert does."

King James reached out and pressed Quinn back against the bed linens. "She's safe for the time being. Rupert has her locked away. He can't take her out of the gaol without someone stopping him."

Quinn wasn't willing to trust anyone with Vivian's safety but himself. "I'll rest a moment more, then I will be going," he assured the king.

A rueful smile came to the king's lips as he moved to stand. He nodded his thanks to the physician as the man left the chamber, closing the door behind him. "Such bravery and strength are why you are one of my magnificent seven."

Quinn didn't feel so strong at the moment, or that his facilities were fully functioning, but he wasn't going to let that stop him from taking advantage of this private audience with the king. "I have something important to tell you, though before I do I need a few concessions from you."

"Tread lightly, Douglas—it sounds like you are threatening your king."

"Not a threat. An arrangement."

When Quinn hesitated, King James waved an impatient hand and added, "I will listen."

"Your life is at stake."

The king blanched and sank to the bed. "Go on."

"Vivian had a vision in which you were killed."

When King James's eyes filled with fear, Quinn wasn't surprised. Vivian had warned him that the king was obsessed with his own early death and superstitious of everyone and everything.

"How and when shall I die?"

"An assassin will strike at a tribunal where you question a woman who is charged with witchcraft. Vivian's vision revealed a young woman with alabaster hair, and that this event would happen in the late afternoon of a night with a full moon. Does that mean anything to you?"

The king's face lost all color. "Bessie Thomson's trial is set for late this afternoon." King James's gaze shifted to the window. "The full moon is tonight." Regaining his composure, he stood once more. "I won't go to the tribunal."

"You must. How else will we know when and where the assassin is to strike?"

King James hauled in a breath and held it a moment, then said, "What about the future Vivian foretold in other visions? She told me I am to be king of both Scotland and England when Elizabeth dies. With our recent accord and with no other heirs in line for the English throne, that vision seemed the most believable."

"If we foil this attempt on your life, those events will play out as they should."

The king made a frustrated sound as he pushed his hand through his hair. "Are you up to the challenge? My life is at stake."

Quinn tested his sword arm, rotating it from his shoulder with moderate, but tolerable pain. "I am."

Through shrewd eyes, the king scanned Quinn's features. He nodded. "Take as many of my men as you need. My entire guard is at your disposal."

Quinn swung his legs over the side of the bed and stood, meeting the king eye-to-eye. "There is still the matter of concessions."

Releasing a weary sigh, the king asked, "What is it you want? I can hardly refuse you anything."

Quinn straightened. "I want you to release Vivian and have all charges against her dismissed."

"I was already working on that task myself, so consider it done. Anything else?"

Quinn nodded. "As part of a personal request, I ask that you rescind Vivian's betrothal to my brother and allow me to marry her instead."

The king raised his brows. "Would Vivian agree to such a proposal?"

"Aye," Quinn answered without hesitation.

The king's lips curved into a slow smile. "Then it shall be done."

Anticipation bloomed, then grew until Quinn felt his strength return. "When does the tribunal start?"

"On the hour."

"Then we'd better talk to your guards and see that everyone is in place before the tribunal begins."

AS THE AFTERNOON light started to fade, the moon could be seen, swollen and glistening in the sky above as Quinn made his way inside the tribunal chamber set up among the ruins of Berwick's old parish church. King James stood beside the accused witch, Bessie Thomson, gathering information from the accused while two judges and a panel of local residents observed.

Quinn noticed a slight trembling in the king's fingers as he read from the paper in his hands. "You are accused of acquiring a charmed ring from Agnes Sampson, which you used to cure your son of an illness he should not have recovered from, and for influencing the behavior of your husband in ways he has reported are not typical for him. How do you plead?" Beads of nervous sweat gathered on King James's forehead as his eyes darted about the room, searching for his would-be attacker.

The young woman beside him was dressed in a simple white gown that was tattered and worn. Her long, white hair made her appear almost ethereal, yet her tears were very real. "I'm innocent, Yer Grace. My only crimes are that of being a loving mother and dedicated wife. Nothing else."

With a quill, King James wrote on the paper he held. When he was done, he lifted his gaze to the accused and asked, "Did you call upon Satan when healing your child?"

The small chamber was crowded, with not only the governing officials and members of the accused's family, but also a dozen members of the king's guard disguised to blend in with other local residents.

Quinn scanned the room impatiently. He wished whoever was going to attack the king would do so. It took everything inside Quinn to stand rigidly still, waiting for events to unfold, when all he wanted was to rush to Vivian's side and release her as the king had promised.

The questioning continued, seemed to drag on, as Quinn concentrated on each member of the crowd. As his gaze lit on the opposite side of the chamber, a prickle of alarm scratched down his spine. The crowd seemed to part. A large man dressed in a pair of ragged, stained breeches and a dirty muslin shirt beneath a homespun tunic shifted forward. In a blur of motion, the man's hand reached beneath the folds of his tunic, producing a blade.

For a heartbeat, Quinn and the man's gazes met until the man's eyes filled with a wild, savage look. He lunged for the king.

Quinn reacted. He surged forward at the same moment and, reaching the king first, Quinn sent King James sprawling on the ground out of harm's way. "Stay down," Quinn ordered.

Waves of shock and tension screamed through the crowd. Those gathered leaned forward as though watching a drama on the stage.

"Bastard king! My daughter is innocent," the dark-haired assailant cried just before Quinn's fist connected with the man's stomach. The attacker's grunt of pain echoed above the chaos. The knife flew from his hand, skidding across the floor and out of reach.

Quinn kept moving forward, using his momentum to take the assailant to the ground. A moment later, the king's guard grabbed the man by the arms and legs, pinning him in place. Even outnumbered and immobilized, the man continued to fight. Spittle foamed on his lips. "Release my child. She's innocent, I tell ye. Innocent."

"Da, nay! Ye'll only make things worse fer all of us." Bessie Thomson dropped to her knees. Her desperate sobs filled the air.

Quinn gained his feet, then quickly moved to the king's side. "Your Grace?" Quinn prompted, holding out his hand.

King James turned to stare at Quinn as though in a haze. "You saved me," the king said, his voice trembling. He took Quinn's hand.

"Of course," Quinn said, pulling the man to his feet. "That was our agreement."

The words seemed to pull the king from his stupor of fear. He straightened, dusted off his coat, and nodded. "You have my thanks and my deepest respect." His lips pulled up in an attempt at a smile. "Now go. Find Vivian. I shall attend you both as soon as I am able."

Without looking back, Quinn exited the parish church, leaving the assassin to the king's guards and quickly made his way to where Vivian was being held.

As the sun faded beneath the horizon, Quinn raced up the stairs and down the long hallway to the guard station. The grim-faced guard watched as Quinn approached. His hand shifted to the hilt of his sword. "State your business," he said with icy precision.

"I am here at the king's request to take Vivian Campbell into my care."

"I have received no such request." The guard drew his sword, his expression as deadly as his tone. "She is a prisoner of Laird Campbell's."

"No longer. King James has acquitted her of all charges. The king's secretary is most efficient, and there has been plenty of time for the order to reach you here." Quinn drew his own sword and motioned with the weapon. "Stand aside and let me pass."

"She is not here."

Quinn's heart stumbled. "Where is she?"

The guard's jaw squared. His eyes caught the glow of the torch on the wall as he lunged forward.

Steel met steel as Quinn countered. His blade touched flesh and came away red. The guard flinched and retreated, but Quinn followed through, catching the man's blade and rolling his wrist. A further twist tore the hilt from the guard's fingers and sent it cartwheeling across the flagstone floor.

In shock and disbelief, the guard waited for Quinn's sword to pierce him through. Instead, Quinn sheathed his blade, but advanced on the guard, grabbing him by the throat and lifting him off his feet. Quinn slammed him against the stone wall. "Where is Vivian?"

The man ineffectively raked at Quinn's hands. "He threatened me . . . He'll kill me . . . if I tell you."

Campbell. Quinn narrowed his gaze. "I'll kill you if you don't."

"I'm not sure I know where she is."

"Think carefully and quickly," Quinn threatened, tightening his hands at the man's throat.

The guard's face turned ashen. "To Castlehill and the place where witches are burned."

"How long ago?"

"Not long. Perhaps half an hour."

Quinn felt as if his heart was being crushed. He forced himself to think past the pain, to ignore the panic that threatened. He released his grip on the man's throat and turned toward the door as the guard crumpled to the floor in a heap.

He might be able to close the distance if he rode like the wind.

Vivian . . .

CHAPTER TWENTY-ONE

WITH A FULL moon overhead and a thousand stars twinkling in the night sky, Quinn made his way to Edinburgh on one of the guard's horses. The horse raced as fast as his legs could carry the two of them through the shadowy landscape.

Quinn could see no more than a dozen or so paces in any direction but instead of heeding the danger, he allowed the well-trained horse his head.

The odds of arriving in time to save Vivian were growing slim. Without divine intervention Quinn was likely to reach Castlehill too late. Fear flashed through him at the thought and he sucked in a breath.

Nay.

He pushed the debilitating thought out of his mind and instead began to pray. Divine intervention was not unheard of. If anyone deserved help from above for all that she had suffered over the years, it was Vivian.

Lord, for once please hear me. Help me. Please don't let me arrive too late. The thought gave him strength and a renewed sense of hope as he pushed himself and his horse to the limits of endurance.

Quinn swept into Edinburgh in record time. In a lather from his exertion, the horse started to slow. "Please, keep it up for a few minutes more," Quinn begged, frustrated by the sense that time was running out.

The horse rallied under Quinn's heels and pushed on, heading toward Castle Rock. The streets were empty—vacant of everyone who might have usually been milling about. Even the guards were absent. Why? Had Rupert threatened them with their own deaths if they stayed to witness what he would do to Vivian? The questions had barely formed when something else drew Quinn's attention. An orange-red glare lit the night sky ahead of him as he crested Castlehill. For a moment Quinn's heart stopped before he realized it was from the torches lighting the way.

Then he heard Vivian scream.

Instead of fear, the sound filled him with joy.

"She's alive!" Together, man and beast roared across the cobbled streets toward the Royal Mile, to the place where others accused of using witchcraft had been burned.

Then he saw them. Flames. Flames were creeping toward Vivian. She was bound to a stake atop a four-foot pile of logs and branches. Flames licked the wood like obscene tongues, devouring the pile with monstrous ferocity. No one else was around. Where was Rupert? Quinn didn't have time to think; he simply acted.

He jumped to the ground, leaving his exhausted horse at

a safe distance, and dashed toward the woman he loved. Heat and smoke blasted his lungs as he made his way toward her. The smoke stung his eyes and seared his lungs, and even so he caught sight of Vivian's face.

Her eyes filled with shock and disbelief. "You're alive!"

Sparks flared, shooting in all directions, and the flames seemed to intensify.

"Quinn!" Vivian's voice was raw with agony.

Death danced all around her. Quinn braced himself against the searing heat and pushed forward. He had to reach her before the flames did. He took two steps toward her when a dagger whizzed past his face, narrowly missing it.

Vivian screamed as she struggled against the bonds that held her.

Quinn drew his sword as Rupert charged, but he was too late as Rupert's fist drove upward into Quinn's jaw.

"You'll not save her! She's mine," Rupert snarled. "I wanted her pain all to myself. I'll never give her up! Never!"

Quinn's sword flew from his hand as he staggered back, his head whipped violently to one side by the blow. His response was instinctual. His left arm lashed out to block a second punch while his right delivered a crushing blow to Rupert's midsection, the power of it lifting the man and hurling him several feet into the darkness.

An explosive curse rent the air as Rupert gained his feet. "She must find absolution in the flames. Only they can purify her soul."

"She's innocent." Quinn's chest heaved as he lunged at Rupert, knocking him off-balance and down to the ground. Quinn retrieved his sword. But before he could fully rise, Rupert gained his feet and rushed forward, dagger drawn.

Rupert caught Quinn off guard, hitting him in the shoulder. Pain erupted and radiated through him, unbalancing Quinn and sending him sprawling to the ground on his back. The impact knocked the sword from his hand and out of reach.

"I will stop you," Quinn warned his opponent. Damn Rupert for torturing Vivian . . . and all the others who came before her. How could one man who was so evil continue to thrive? "What you do is not justice. It's murder." Quinn quickly regained his feet.

"Perhaps, but only to those with the blackest of hearts." Rupert smiled evilly. "You should have stayed away. Now your black heart will burn alongside your witch's!"

Rupert charged with a dagger in his hand.

FIRE! THE FLAMES were licking at Vivian's feet, soon to devour her. She couldn't breathe. She struggled against the bonds at her wrists, ankles, and waist. But even in her tortured state, joy pulsed through her.

Quinn was alive!

Moonlight polished Quinn's hair to a bright ebony and

lit his features with bold clarity. Despite the smoke, she could see his eyes were bright in his soot-stained face.

Giddy tears replaced her grief-stricken ones at the sight of the man she loved. The love in her heart swelled, overcoming the heat of the fire. She'd loved Quinn from the moment she'd looked into his eyes.

Never in her life had she felt anything like she did with Quinn. Her heart beat wildly at his approach. Her spirit soared. She was in love with him. Honestly and completely in love. She didn't want to die, not when everything in her life had at last come right. She wanted to live to bear his children. To have a life together in peace as Quinn had longed for. To lay her hand against his cheek once more and tell him that she loved him.

Nay, she couldn't die like this. Not without letting Quinn know.

Vivian wrestled against her bindings, again and again, to no avail. She could feel herself weakening, feel the smoke draining her strength with each labored breath. The heat beneath her became more and more intense as the flames grew ever closer. It wouldn't be long before her dress caught fire, and then it would all be over.

Out of the shadows, Rupert surged forward, attacking Quinn, taking him to the ground. "Nay!" Vivian's heart clogged her throat.

Quinn stood. He grabbed Rupert's hand that held the dagger, then twisted behind the man, kicking Rupert in the back, sending him lurching forward.

Rupert hissed, his eyes flaring an instant before they widened.

It was then Vivian realized Rupert's wrist had been turned during his lurch. The dagger in his hands was now embedded in his own chest.

Rupert howled in pain. "This is not how it is to end."

Quinn pulled the dagger free from Rupert's chest. Without hesitation, Quinn turned toward her, racing toward the flames.

Smoke stung her eyes, seared her lungs as the flames caught the hem of her gown. She tried to cry out, but no sound emerged from her chest. Life was draining away as the fire stole the air from her lungs.

Vivian struggled to remain conscious. A streak of color approached her. Her legs buckled, gave way. She felt herself falling into the flames. A heartbeat later, a wash of cool air touched her cheeks, a welcome relief. She sucked in a gulp of smoke-free air, then coughed, convulsing as a pair of arms held her. Hands batted her legs, then the hem of her skirt. "It's all right, Vivian. I've got you."

Quinn! His words rippled over her like a silken caress that touched her all the way to her soul. She drew in another breath. Her vision cleared until she saw his anguished face above her own.

"I thought I'd lost you," he said, his voice raw as he moved them farther away from the flames and billowing smoke. "You're safe."

Vivian's heart pounded wildly, painfully. A dark shadow lurched forward. A scream caught in her throat. A broadsword came slashing in an arc toward Quinn's head. Her cry had alerted him, because Quinn twisted. The steel missed his neck and shoulder, slicing harmlessly through the fabric of his tunic instead.

Rupert recovered. He charged again, his eyes blazing hell's wrath. "Damn you both!"

Quinn's arms moved softly around her. He remained where he was. Why didn't he move? Why didn't he set her down and defend himself?

Vivian's heart stopped. Rupert drew near.

Suddenly Quinn leapt to the side, taking her with him, moving them both out of harm's way. Rupert, unable to stop his momentum, charged past them and straight into the raging pyre. The four-foot stack of wood caved in on Rupert, burying him in flames. His scream echoed in the stillness of the night as he collapsed against the wood and flames. Was he unconscious? Because he lay there, making no effort to break free.

Vivian pressed her hands to her mouth as she watched Rupert's clothing catch fire. In the next moment he was fully aflame.

Quinn set her on her feet and charged forward. She nearly collapsed from the sudden lack of support, but forced her knees to lock, holding herself upright as she watched Quinn pull Rupert's body from the inferno. Quinn dragged the charred body free then set Rupert on the ground, tamping out the remaining flames.

Vivian staggered forward, dropping to her knees beside both men. "Rupert?" He was covered in blood and soot and black, peeling skin. She had to do something to heal him, to stop the pain he must be feeling.

Rupert's face contorted. His eyes turned to her, glittering brightly in the glare of the fire. "Don't want . . . your pity."

She should hate this man before her, hate him for all the suffering he'd caused her, his father, his mother, Quinn, and so many others. But she couldn't. She dredged up the words she knew she must say. "I forgive you."

Rupert's eyes widened. "Why?"

"Forgiveness is not witchcraft but it can do magical things." Saying the words made Vivian breathe easier. Forgiveness was the right path to take.

"May God be with you," Quinn said to Rupert. "May he show you the mercy you never showed anyone else."

Quinn came up behind her and enfolded her in his arms while the cool air of the night settled around them. She and Quinn remained with Rupert until his breathing ceased. When he was finally gone, her whole body started to shake.

Quinn pulled her close and simply held her until her shaking stopped. Finally, when she felt more in control, she pulled back and said, "Thank you, for taking me on this journey. For coming for me tonight." She looked up at

Quinn and felt tears form in her eyes. Not tears of sadness this time but tears of joy. "I love you," she said, giving voice to the words she'd thought she might never have the chance to say.

He smiled down at her, filling the darkness so she could see nothing but moonlight highlighting his face, could feel nothing but his presence. "You were more than worth the journey. I would traverse hell itself for you. I will come for you in your hour of need anywhere, anytime." His gaze was tender, adoring. "I love you, Vivian."

The words sent longing into her heart. The pain of the last few hours melted away until it felt as though she and Quinn were the only two people in the world.

She closed her eyes and took a deep breath of the cool night air. She heard the pop and hiss of the fire, but beyond that was the silence of the night. An errant breeze pushed to her the scent of heather in the distance.

She drew another breath, letting it slide through her. "Is it really over?"

"Aye. Tomorrow all this will only be a memory, and we will start anew." His lips brushed hers, as if testing to make certain she was real and not just a dream.

And yet she still felt vulnerable and afraid. Any moment now she expected others who hunted witches to find her and pull her away from what she had come to love and need in her life.

Quinn.

For the past several years she'd wanted to be in charge of her own life, to make her own decisions. She'd tried so hard to avoid the mistakes her parents had made that she'd only allowed herself to dream of living in a small cottage in a village where she would help others, healing them with her skills, finding happiness in a simple life.

And be very much alone.

Her heart stumbled painfully in her chest. She wasn't sure when it happened, or how, but suddenly she knew she didn't want those things anymore. All because of Quinn.

The man before her was nothing like her father. Quinn didn't try to dominate her or steer her thoughts in a direction of his choosing. He allowed her to be herself, to express her own thoughts, and be her own person. He believed that what she did to heal others was a gift, and that her visions were not a curse but a blessing. He accepted who she was without trying to change her.

"What about tomorrow?" she asked Quinn, feeling tears well in her eyes before they slipped down her cheeks.

He took her hand in his and placed them both over his heart. She saw the love in his eyes, the way he looked at her as if she were his heart and soul. And yet she still belonged to another.

"Don't be afraid of tomorrow." He bent to kiss the damp trail of tears on her cheeks. "Marry me, Vivian. I want to start each day by seeing your face beside me when I wake. I want to hear your voice at night when I go to bed. Let me plait your hair for you in the afternoon, and we'll catch fish together in the evening, side-by-side. I want to watch you cradle our children in your arms. I want to grow a garden filled with the herbs you need to keep those we love healthy and well. I want to keep you safe in my castle yet protect you all the remaining days of my life." He gazed at her, his eyes dark and bottomless, and filled with infinite hope. "Do you want those things as well?"

"I want all those things and so much more, but can we truly reach for what is not ours to take?"

"A very good question," a voice boomed from the darkness behind them.

Quinn tensed and pulled back but did not release his grip on her hand. As they turned, the darkness seemed to part and a horse and rider moved closer. Beneath the moonlight she could see the man was familiar, yet she had never seen him before. Then she understood. Where Quinn had dark hair, his was blond. Where Quinn had dark, soulful eyes, his were a startling blue.

"I believe introductions are in order," Reid said, dismounting. He strode toward them, hesitating only slightly as his gaze lit on Rupert's charred remains. Reid stopped before them and offered a bow. "Reid Douglas, the Earl of Douglas. You obviously know my brother, Quinn. And I believe you are Vivian Campbell. My betrothed." Reid's eyes suddenly filled with challenge as he turned to his brother. "Are you forcing yourself on what is mine?"

"I'm not forcing anything," Quinn replied, then asked with a frown, "How did you know to come to Edinburgh instead of the prison?"

"I rode there first and was redirected by one of the guards. The man seemed eager to send me after you once he saw the army I brought with me. Sorry I wasn't here sooner," Reid said, shifting his gaze once more to Rupert's charred remains.

"When have you even been on time for a fight?"

Vivian tried to swallow the dry, tight lump in her throat. "Quinn, Reid, please—" She looked at Quinn, but he wasn't looking at her anymore. His gaze was on Reid, his mouth tight.

"You haven't spoken with King James yet, I take it," Quinn asked, tightening his fingers around hers.

"Not since the betrothal documents were signed." Reid's eyes narrowed, focusing intensely on his brother.

"Why are you here? Why now?" Quinn asked through gritted teeth.

"You sent for me and my men. 'Twas my understanding you needed my help to save the day?"

Quinn made a sound that was close to a laugh. "You're a little late on that count, Brother."

This had gone on long enough. Vivian reached up and touched Quinn's cheek. They had averted one disaster tonight, they did not need to hurl themselves headfirst into yet another with his brother. "We both forgave Rupert this night for all the evil things he'd done to us. Perhaps we can extend that same mercy to your brother who has done nothing wrong?"

"You're right." The tension eased from Quinn's body.

Vivian turned to face his brother. "Laird Douglas, it is a pleasure to meet you. I wish the circumstances were not so difficult, but there is no skirting that issue. The truth is, I do not wish to marry you. My heart belongs to your brother." She brought their entwined hands to her lips and kissed Quinn's hand. She felt the gentle strength in his touch and savored it. Tears of happiness filled her eyes. The same emotion swelled in her chest, filled her heart to overflowing.

"It was not my intention to hurt you, Reid," Quinn added. "I found Vivian as you had requested and prepared to bring her back to you as we'd planned, but circumstances forced us to take a different journey. Somewhere along the way a part of me that I'd denied for so long came back to life and I fell in love with your promised bride."

Quinn dropped his gaze to his and Vivian's entwined fingers. "I love you, Brother. I always will. I've fought at your side for so many years, risking everything for king and country, but I don't want that anymore. I want to fight for Vivian, for our love, for our family yet to come." He fixed his gaze upon Reid. "I violated your trust not just with what happened between us, but I also asked King James to rescind your betrothal and to marry Vivian to me."

Reid's gaze had not wavered from Quinn's face while his

brother talked. It did not waver now as Reid clenched his fists and walked slowly forward, stopping before the two of them.

Quinn dropped her hand and tensed as though preparing to fight.

Reid reached for his brother's arms, clasped them tight, then smiled. "You've told me more than I deserve to hear. I can blame no one for the situation but myself. If I had come for Vivian . . . who knows what might have happened instead." He shrugged.

Quinn pulled his brother to him and clapped him on the back as the tension in the air lessened. "You can dream whatever dream you want, but I choose to believe that Vivian would still be mine."

The two men laughed as they separated. "Does your fine bride-to-be have a sister by any chance?"

Both men looked at her.

Despite the reconciliation between the two men, Vivian frowned. "Nay, I have no sister, but you are both forgetting I have not yet given my answer to Quinn's proposal."

Reid's brow rose in question. "Because you changed your mind now that you've met me?"

"Because you interrupted us." Quinn's smile faded and his expression became grave. He took Vivian's hands in his once more. "What is it? What's wrong?"

"Would you like my answer?"

"More than anything as long as it is aye." The very air

around them shivered as Quinn looked into her eyes. "I came so close to losing you tonight. I can't bear the thought of being apart from you again. Not even for a moment. I love you and ask that you join your life to mine."

Vivian rose up on her toes, bringing her lips to his, answering him with her kiss. Her kiss said it all—*I want you, I need you, I love you.* Eventually she drew back, and smiled as she raised their joined hands to cover his heart. "My heart is yours and yours is mine."

"For all eternity." He kissed her again with the promise of forever between them.

"It won't be nearly long enough," she said, smiling through the sheen of tears blinding her.

"Never enough," he agreed as the sound of hoofbeats on the cobblestones broke through the silence of the night. They stepped apart and turned to see Moreis, Lachlan and behind them the men who no doubt made up Reid's army approaching. Another man, who could be none other than Malcolm Hamilton, if his swarthy complexion were any indication, rode beside Lachlan.

Malcolm bowed his head in greeting. "My apologies for arriving so late to this fight. My army and I were not at Falkirk, but Lachlan tracked us down and here we are at your request."

"It was a risk to assume you were in residence," Quinn acknowledged. "Everything worked out as it should have in the end. I thank you for coming all this way."

Malcolm struck his chest with his fist once in a salute. "'Tis what we each do for the other that makes us brothers-in-arms. Aye?"

"Aye," Quinn echoed, returning the salute.

"All these warriors can now escort you safely home." Reid waved his hand toward the assembled men. "I assume you will head for Kinmount House in Dumfriesshire instead of Redhouse Castle?"

Quinn looked at Vivian with longing in his eyes. "Do you want to go home, Vivian?"

"Nothing would make me happier."

CHAPTER TWENTY-TWO

VIVIAN TOOK A breath and let the scene before her sink into her soul. From the parapets, she looked upon her new home. The home she would share with Quinn. She never imagined she would feel so comfortable in a place she'd never been before, but she did.

Kinmount House was not as demure as its name suggested. It was no house but a fortress whose blue-gray stone walls were as strong as they were beautiful. From the reddish-gold bracken and dark green ivy that climbed the walls, to the gardens that spilled over in a riot of color, her new home had brought her nothing but joy, especially today when she would join her life to Quinn's.

She looked below to the lists, where she should have heard the clanging of swords as her betrothed's men trained for battle. Instead, the outer yard had been set up with tables, laden with food, with servants scurrying to and fro, preparing the feast that would follow the exchanging of their vows in the chapel. She and Quinn had wanted to celebrate afterward with friends and family outside, bathed in the glory of the sun's rays, reminding them that they had survived the darkness. The future ahead would be filled with nothing but light.

Near the chapel their guests gathered. Moreis and Gillis had been inseparable since their arrival at Kinmount House. Vivian had given her faithful maid the gemstones she had hidden in her skirt. Gillis in turn had given them back, saying she did not need anything more than the treasure she'd already found in the company of her new friends and family at the castle.

Lachlan had flourished since their return as well. Quinn had noted that the young man seemed more confident about his swordsmanship since their return as he'd proven in the lists against the castle's warriors and especially under Malcolm Hamilton's tutelage. Today, Lachlan smiled and laughed as he strolled the grounds with Sisters Genevieve and Collette on his arms. All the sisters from Inishail Convent and many other guests had come to wish her and Quinn joy on this, their wedding day.

Tears of happiness sprang to Vivian's eyes as she turned to the man beside her. "Can you believe we made it to this moment?"

"I never doubted we would survive. Not for a moment."

She smiled at her soon-to-be husband. "I love you so much."

"And I love you," Quinn said as he reached up and smoothed an errant strand of her hair away from her cheek. For this, their wedding day, Vivian wore her hair down around her shoulders with a spray of flowers as a crown about her head. Her gown, made from the palest green silk, trimmed in seed pearls and embroidered with scrolling green and gold leaves, was a gift from the king.

Quinn's tunic was the same color as her gown. In his finest clothes, he was so handsome she wondered if she would actually remember the words of her vows when the time came during the ceremony.

"Thank you for bringing me here, Quinn. Your home is so peaceful. I know I will be happy here."

"Not my home, our home." Quinn bent to kiss her.

A door opened and closed off to their right. "The two of you are a sight to behold."

Quinn pulled back but did not release her at the sound of King James's voice. Stopping before them, the king held out a bouquet of flowers to her.

"We are honored, Your Grace, that you would come to our wedding." Vivian smiled and accepted the flowers from her guardian. In the years she had known him, time had woven gray into his hair and lined his face. New wrinkles had appeared at the corners of his eyes since he'd started his witch tribunals. No doubt more lines would gather along with the others in the years ahead.

"They are almost ready for you at the chapel," the king said, "but I wanted a moment alone with you both. Quinn, I owe you my life. It is a debt of honor I shall never forget."

Quinn bowed his head. "It was an honor to serve, and I

shall continue to do so in a limited fashion."

The king nodded as he turned to Vivian. "I put you through so much, far more than you deserved, and for that, I am sorry."

"We cannot go back and change the past, but what about the others who have been falsely accused of witchcraft? Can you do something to help them?" The words were out before she could stop them. Vivian bit her lip, fearing the king's response.

He released a heavy sigh. "Rupert is gone. I will not replace him with another who is filled with such hatred, I can promise you that. And I will do everything in my power to discern the truth from those accused in a more humane way."

His concession was more than she'd hoped for. She prayed it would be enough. "Thank you, Your Grace."

Quinn addressed the king. "If you are concerned with Vivian's welfare in the future then I ask one more thing of you."

King James's brows slanted down, knowing he could hardly refuse given his previous sentiments of sorrow and support. "What might that be?"

"I ask that you make Kinmount House a place of sanctuary. No one within its walls can be arrested for witchcraft as long as you sit on the throne."

The king's look became one of bewilderment. "What if there is a witch among your people?"

"Then trust me to handle the matter."

The king frowned. "It is highly unusual."

"I have been your faithful servant for many years. Time and again I have proven my loyalty. I ask now for your trust in return."

"And you believe me granting such will keep Vivian safe?"

Quinn nodded. "I will protect her with every resource at my disposal and with my life, should it be necessary."

The king's lips thinned, but eventually his head bobbed in consent. "Consider it done. I will have the papers drawn up on my return to Edinburgh."

"Thank you," Quinn said, bowing.

The king stepped forward and placed a kiss on Vivian's cheek. "Now, we must go to the chapel. I have delayed your wedding long enough." He turned, not waiting for the two of them to follow, and made his way belowstairs.

Quinn put his arm around Vivian's waist and tilted her toward him. "I can see it in your eyes that you wished for more from King James."

"While in gaol, I heard sounds I shall never forget." Vivian shuddered. "The prisoners were tortured to the point of admitting anything simply to make their anguish stop. There is no truth or justice in that. So many of those falsely accused will be executed regardless of the king's words of mercy."

Quinn's gaze was a warm caress. "Fear not, Vivian. The king has already given us a solution to that problem. With sanctuary given to Kinmount House by the king, we will gather those who fear for their lives before they are falsely accused and bring them here. We will spread the word far and wide that this is a place of refuge."

Vivian laughed. "You are devious, Quinn Douglas, but I love you all the more for it."

"I will do whatever it takes to see you and others like you are safe."

"I thought you didn't believe in witches."

"I don't," Quinn replied. "But I do believe in magic."

Filled with hope for a better future for those who were different, Vivian rose up on her toes, and with her lips hovering close to Quinn's she asked, "Shall we make our guests wait a little bit longer?"

"Nothing would make me happier." With a gleam of mischief in his eyes, he kissed her.

The End

Author's Note

All facts regarding King James VI of Scotland (later King James I of England) and his involvement with the North Berwick witch trials are accurate, based on my research. As for his character, a good deal had to come from my imagination about this controversial king.

James came to the throne at the age of thirteen months. An early childhood illness left him almost unable to walk. James overcame his disability but because it was impossible for him to fully enjoy outdoor sports such as riding or hunting, he devoted his time and energy to books and scholarly studies instead. The events of his early childhood might also account for James's fear of the unknown. As he grew older, he was also terrified of a violent death.

James's interest in witchcraft began around the same time as his marriage to Princess Anne of Denmark. At this time witchcraft was not a popular topic of discussion in Scotland or England. It was a matter of intense interest in Denmark and adjacent countries, which were suffering from the throes of an outbreak of witch mania. Witches were being outed by accusers across Denmark, and the people were terrified of Satan's agents. Witches were looked upon as slaves of Satan, compelled to do his bidding.

The marriage between James and Anne took place on August 20, 1589 in Denmark. James was not present; George Keith, the Fifth Earl Marischal, stood in as his proxy. Shortly after the marriage, Anne took a ship to Scotland to be with her new husband, but foul weather, and a series of mishaps forced the vessel to take shelter in a port on the coast of Norway. When James heard of the great storm that had driven back Anne's ship, he sailed from Scotland to Norway to claim his bride personally. His own crossing of the sea was uncommonly stormy. Coupled with the trouble Anne had encountered in her efforts to reach Scotland, the events seemed uncanny to the superstitious James. Yet a third storm struck his ship and almost wrecked the vessel as he brought his young bride home to Edinburgh in the spring of 1590. James was convinced that witches had used black magic to keep Anne out of Scotland.

Later that same year when accusations of witchcraft were made in the village of North Berwick, James took a personal interest in the proceedings. He was present at many of the interrogations of several of the accused and became convinced that not only was witchcraft real, but that it had been used on him personally. He was determined that the crimes against him be punished. A sense of justice motivated James, as well as the superstition that those who prosecuted witchcraft using the law were the ones most protected by God from its ill effects. By prosecuting the simple Scottish commoners in and around North Berwick, James believed he was ensuring the safety of himself and his wife. His experience with the North Berwick witches led James to write a book on witchcraft and the supernatural, which he titled *Demonology*.

More than a hundred women and men were arrested, and many of them subjected to horrifying tortures to extract confessions to a whole range of crimes, including treason against the Scottish crown. The Berwick trials dragged on for two years. In the end, some seventy men and women were convicted of witchcraft and treason. It is not known how many were executed, but the form of execution for witches in Scotland was burning at the stake. Usually the condemned were strangled to death as an act of mercy before being burned.

When James became King of England in 1603 *Demonology* was republished. One of his initial actions as the English monarch was to revise the witchcraft statute of England, by making its penalties much more severe than was the case with the old witchcraft act that had been in use under Elizabeth I. Crimes that had been punishable by a term of prison became, under James, punishable by death.

Toward the end of his life, James's belief in witches and witchcraft began to falter as he became aware of several instances in which those who had accused their neighbors of witchcraft later confessed to having lied under oath and fabricated the charges.

All these events had a profound effect on the people and the society of Great Britain. It is believed Shakespeare adapted parts of the North Berwick witch trials—including the torture rituals—into the plot of *Macbeth*. The North Berwick witch trials were the first major witchcraft trials in Scotland, but many followed, claiming an estimated total of 3,000 to 4,000 lives between 1560 and 1707.

Agnes Sampson, Euphemia Maclean, Norma Croft, and Bessie Thomson, named as witches in this book, were all accused, tried, and executed as witches as part of the witch trials in Scotland.

Margaret Aitken was charged as a witch, but to spare her own life during her confession she claimed to be able to recognize other witches by looking for a special mark in their eyes. Her claim spared her life but condemned many innocent women to their death on her testimony. After four months of identifying witches, she was exposed as a fraud and burned at the stake. In *Seven Nights with a Scot*, I moved the time period of Margaret's actions from 1597 to 1591 in order to save Quinn.

Finally, I used the Cayton Caves near Beckbury, Shropshire, England as a model for the cavern which Vivian and Quinn used to hide from Rupert. The cave complex is hidden three feet beneath a farmer's field. The original purpose and date of the man-made caves are disputed, though the most commonly held belief is that they date from the late eighteenth century to early nineteenth century. The Cayton Caves were simply too perfect a place for Quinn and Vivian to find a night of reprieve so I moved them to the sixteenth century and to Gargunnock, Scotland, and added Downie's Loup as a means of escape for the purposes of this book.

While the witch trials were a terrible period in Scottish and eventually English history, I choose to believe there were heroes amongst the people who worked for changes not only to the laws of the time, but also to help others in need of protection and care. *Seven Nights with a Scot* and the others books in The King's Men series are filled with men and women who do just that. The stories are a combination of reality, fantasy, and dreams for a better tomorrow.

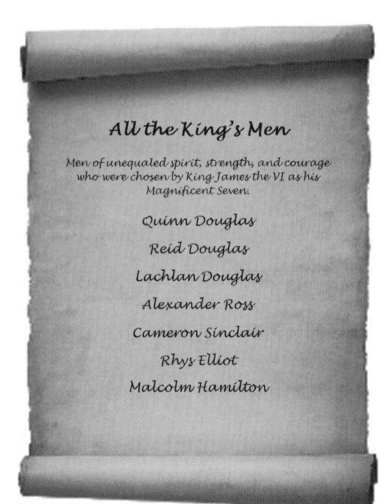

All the King's Men

Men of unequaled spirit, strength, and courage who were chosen by King James the VI as his Magnificent Seven.

Quinn Douglas

Reid Douglas

Lachlan Douglas

Alexander Ross

Cameron Sinclair

Rhys Elliot

Malcolm Hamilton

If you enjoyed *Seven Nights with a Scot*, you'll love the next book in....

All the Kings Men series

Book 1: *Seven Nights with A Scot*

Book 2: *Romancing the Laird*

Book 3: *Coming soon*

About the Author

Gerri Russell is the award-winning author of historical and contemporary novels including the Brotherhood of the Scottish Templars series and *Flirting with Felicity*. A two-time recipient of the Romance Writers of America's Golden Heart Award and winner of the American Title II competition sponsored by *RT Book Reviews* magazine, she is best known for her adventurous and emotionally intense novels set in the thirteenth- and fourteenth-century Scottish Highlands. Before Gerri followed her passion for writing romance novels, she worked as a broadcast journalist, a newspaper reporter, a magazine columnist, a technical writer and editor, and an instructional designer. She lives in the Pacific Northwest with her husband and four mischievous black cats.

Thank you for reading

Seven Nights with a Scot

If you enjoyed this book, you can find more from all our great authors at TulePublishing.com, or from your favorite online retailer.

TULE
PUBLISHING

Made in the USA
Middletown, DE
05 September 2019